The Wonders of a Woman

Delia Nicole

DEDICATION

To our ancestors who were not allowed to read and write, but still mastered the art of knowledge sharing through verbal storytelling.

LOVE

PASSION

SEX

DECEIT

Love

HOUSE PEST

I was miserable and had grown to hate this place. The crazy thing was, I was uneasy in my own home, like a guest, an unwanted visitor, or a pest. However, it was my home . . . at least it had been before my mom allowed him in. We were already at capacity with my mom, sister, and me living in a small one-bedroom apartment. A fourth wheel, he was unwanted—at least by me. My little sister was young and seemed unbothered, but I, a pre-teen, was very bothered. And my mom? Well, my mom was over-the-moon happy, as if she'd won a prize. I'm still unsure of what she saw in him.

They met at her job, coworkers— strike number one. He was married but separated with eight kids amongst six women—strike two. And he was missing his top four teeth—strikeout! She should have taken a hard pass on this fool. I immediately noticed him 'coming to spend time with my mom' quickly led to dinner with our family and staying afterward for longer and longer periods of time.

This turned into him staying overnight from time to time; he claimed it was "too late" to commute by train back to his place. This befuddled me because my mom did not have a room; she slept on the pull-out couch, and the bedroom was me and my sister's.

Fast-forward a couple of months, and he had taken up residence with us. My mother was on cloud nine, and I was thoroughly displeased. Shortly after, he lost his job. While he laid up on the couch, sucking up the air, lights, and food, my mom went from struggling to take care of three to struggling to take care of four and hunting for a second job. I never once saw him open the classifieds. I remember asking my mom why he wasn't looking for work. Unfortunately, I was told *I was a child, and I wouldn't understand; things were complicated and tough for him.*

I heard him laugh and call out for my mom to make sure I "stayed in a child's place."

Our lives were no longer ours. He didn't eat pork, so we no longer could. He had a severe nut allergy, so we could no longer have our favorite snacks. He was a Jehovah's Witness, so we could no longer celebrate birthdays or holidays. I, with my sister in tow, spent as much time as possible away from the apartment.

From school, we went to the library and did our homework, dropped in at home for a snack, which was scarce because he ate up everything, then it was outside or to a friend's house until it was time to shower and go to bed.

One day after school, I turned my key in the lock of the front door and was met with the security chain. I banged on the door, and he walked up, partially clothed, and told us we needed to come back later before he pushed the door shut and locked the door. Unlocking it again, I shoved it open and, through the four-inch gap created by the chain, saw a female run across the living room toward OUR bedroom.

Pissed that I tried to re-enter, he slammed the door so hard that the heavy steel hit my face, busting my nose, and caused my sister to fall backward. With tears, and a blood-soaked shirt, my sister and I ran the eleven blocks to my mother's job to tell her everything. She cleaned me up and sent us to our grandma's house until she got off work, promising to handle him when she got home. I was so happy to end this nightmare.

The next morning, I woke up happy for a fresh start and almost shit my pants when I walked out of my room. He was on the couch watching TV with my mom, smiling and laughing. I was in shock. My mom said, "Good morning, baby," like nothing had happened the day before. My nose was still bruised, so I knew it wasn't a dream.

He looked at me, smirked, and said, "How's your nose, kiddo?"

My mom hugged me and explained some bullshit story he had fed her about what happened, and honestly, I wasn't sure if I hated her or felt sorry for her.

One Saturday night, I heard my mom sobbing gently in the bathroom. I cracked open the door, entered, and approached her in a delicate manner. My heart broke for her because I knew she deserved better, even though I was convinced she did not know this herself. I whispered, "Mommy, what's wrong?"

"It's gone." She stated through teary eyes.

"Mommy, what's gone?" I whispered.

While she gathered herself to speak, my heart fluttered on the inside. My mind started racing. Maybe he found another woman and left us!

Maybe he went to the store for a pack of cigarettes and a Pepsi like my Uncle Bernard and never made it back. Six years later, my aunt and cousins still looked for him. They had filed a missing person's report and everything. I overheard my auntie Carolyn say she once saw Uncle Bernard at Coney Island with a Spanish woman and a biracial-looking boy who appeared to be around eight or nine years old. Aunt Carolyn said she would never tell her sister this news and just supported her as she followed up quarterly with law enforcement to see if any new developments had been made.

I secretly hoped we got lucky, and he pulled an Uncle Bernard on us. No such luck. What he did pull was larceny. My mother's tax return, in addition to the money she had saved for the past year to get us a larger apartment so she could get off that couch, had disappeared. This was a time that I wished my mom understood the importance of having a bank account, $3,829 gone.

The door locked turned, and shockingly, he walked through the door. Running to my room and back, I gave my mom our aluminum bat she kept under my bed. I knew a head would get cracked open tonight. He walked into our living room and dropped to his knees, sobbing. This woman who I no longer recognized as my mother ran to him, asking him what was wrong. He babbled some bullshit about trying to double our money gambling at a poker game and lost all of it. I ran into the living room, eagerly handing her the bat. "Put that up, honey" she responded quietly.

Assuming that was too messy, while my baby sister was watching, I ran and got the phone, dialed it, then handed it to her. My mom looked at me in shock as I shoved the phone to her ear. I kept hearing the 9-1-1 operator saying, "9-1-1, what is your emergency?"

My mom spoke into the phone and looked at me deliberately and said, "Sorry, ma'am, there is no emergency. We misdialed." A lone tear dropped down my cheek, and I took my shattered heart into my room.

Mommy was in love. Deeply. I did not understand it, refused to accept it, and wouldn't acknowledge it. I knew from her past, love was something she craved. Being abandoned by her mother, rejected by her father, and betrayed by her ex-husband caused this conundrum. This insufferable love led her down a path of self-hate and tolerance of exploited love. It was a love she yearned for that my sister, and I could not fulfill. We loved her. In our eyes, she was a supernatural being he slowly turned into a mortal.

Waiting until my mom's next day off, I approached her while she and my little sister were cooking, to ask if we could talk in private. He came into the kitchen and barked, "No, I'm hungry.

You'll have to talk to your mom after I eat."

I wanted to throw the pot of boiling water on his toothless ass, but my mom pleaded, "After we eat, baby." Irritated I walked away.

I couldn't eat; I was disgusted. The way he was smacking and chewing with food on his face and crumbs on his shirt, slurping and belching? Ugh. Everything annoyed me. He gulped his drink down quickly and started to choke. I looked at him, thinking, *Good for your greedy ass!* My mom patted him on his back, but his choking became more violent, and his eyes started to bulge. He reached up, clawing at his throat, and began to wheeze. My mom yelled and screamed for us to call for help.

When he fell out of the chair, and lost consciousness, I grabbed my sister and the phone and ran into our bedroom. I was scared; I had never seen someone convulse as violently as he had. I dialed 9-1-1 while my mom hysterically performed CPR, yelling out that help was on the way.

Minutes later, my mom walked into the room, defeated, and whispered, "He's dead."

I felt terrified. I sobbed and thought of how frightening this had to be for my baby sister. When I pulled her close, I noticed the empty bag of crushed peanuts inside her trash can.

AT LONG LAST

$\mathscr{T}$hough Lee had been on an airplane several times in his life, this long ride had only occurred two times before.

He had known from the first time they walked hand in hand down the hot, dusty Mississippi road, and he described into her wide, wondrous eyes all the things he had seen that he wanted to show her this place. He knew that he wanted to stand beneath the Arc de Triumph and simply, silently look. No words would be necessary as they contemplated the architecture together, quietly remarking on the smoothness of the lines and the amazing detail. Quaint cafes would line the streets interspersed with little boutiques full of tiny and expensive items, antiques, keepsakes, and even souvenirs. Sunsets would sparkle and glisten on the world-famous Seine River as couples walked alongside speaking in words unfamiliar but pleasing to his ears.

The last time he was here, most of his days were far less picturesque. Most of his time was spent with his fellow soldiers at camp. But one day, shortly before they were scheduled to ship out home and before his separation from the service, he had some R-and-R time in the rear available and went to the city. At this point, he didn't even know Iris, but when he walked down those streets, he saw the soft lighting and smelled the city, it was as though he fell in love with it.

Years later, when he held Iris's small, brown hand, sitting on the porch enjoying the company and the breeze, he was transported to that place as he fell in love with her. He had always wanted to bring these two loves, his wife and the City of Love, together. Now, here they were, heading to Paris together at last.

Iris always said he would talk to a brick wall. With so many air miles and hours in front of them, he made at least three new best friends.

All his seat neighbors had heard the story of Lee and Iris' first meeting. He was friends with Iris' brother and went to his house to join him at a party. When he asked if Lou was there, she responded, "No, but I am. You can take me instead." It was unusual at that time for a woman to be so forthright. Lee found out later that she had her eye on him for a few weeks, but he was moving too slow. He was smitten. His seat neighbor to the right heard all about their abrupt emigration to Gary with their brother and his new wife.

The seats to the right heard about the recent travels Lee and Iris had been on together. They had visited so many places that were important in their individual and collective lives. From former homes and family homes, places they shared laughs and places they shared tears, he had slowly and deliberately spent the last two months visiting across the country. Lee was amazed at how some of the places had changed and at how some of them had stayed remarkably the same. He knew there was a small piece of himself and Iris in each. He shared these stories with his neighbors but kept a few of their most precious stories for himself. They were his treasure.

Lee's neighbor across the aisle saw every picture of their children and grandchildren in his new smartphone. He was super proud of learning how to use all the features on his phone, and besides, they had plenty of time. Without even seeing her face, he knew Iris was rolling her eyes but smiling at his constant talking. He loved to talk and get to know people, but Iris had always been much quieter.

Finally, after many others on the plane had started to doze and the cabin lights were low, he leaned his head back and thought about how blessed he was with sixty-five years of marriage. In his dreams, he saw his beloved bride grow from a short, slim teenager to a beautiful, articulate, capable grown woman, wife, and mother, then into her elder years. She had only grown more lovely over time. Their love grew exponentially with each year. How had he ended up joined in matrimony to this lovely, classy, strong, fireball of a woman? He couldn't believe the hand that life had dealt them. The heartbreaks were well worth the multitude of blessings.

Moving slowly due to age, but consistently because he was determined, Lee took Iris to see so many of the beautiful sights.

Some he had seen years before, many he had seen on tv, but all he gazed upon with wonder now that he had added age, life experiences, and of course, his beloved to the scene. Even after staying for an entire week, it wasn't long enough. He knew this trip would never be long enough for him.

"We have had a wonderful trip," he remarked offhandedly. Sharing the beauty of this city and the experience of traveling overseas with his love was even more powerful than he could have imagined. At this point, the only view that he could see was the mishmash of lights shining out over the beautiful river through his tired and now-teary eyes. As they stood on the bridge with the Seine flowing gently below them, he thought about all the different phases of life they had witnessed and experienced together.

The overt, dangerous racism of Mississippi that, along with his fear of the snakes that were also plentiful there, encouraged them to make a move up to the northern country of Gary. They persevered through the more subtle, but just as cutting racism that met them in Indiana. He thought about the birth and raising of their three kids. These were some of the happiest years of his life. They had enjoyed their children's childhoods, shared pride at every accomplishment. Together, they had buried one of their beloved children, and despite thinking their individual hearts would break, they stayed strong for each other. He thought about the grandchildren who they spoiled together, watched grow together, and now watched them have their own children. Sixty-five years of marriage was a miracle in and of itself.

Lee swiped at his face, trying to bat the tears away, but knowing that even after all the tears that he had cried, there were plenty left to shed for her. Swallowing the huge lump in his throat, he twisted the top of the beautiful container he carried to every destination.

"I'm so sorry, Iris. So, so sorry. I should have brought you here long ago. You deserved to see everything in this big, beautiful world. You deserved to know that nothing in it could compare to you. I hope you always knew . . ." He had to stop talking again. By now, tears dripped from his face as though he was personally supplying a rainstorm.

He looked at his bracelet. It had been specially made for him. One heart-shaped charm with a picture of his beloved Iris in a heart-shaped frame bordered in gold, a sixty-five indicating each blissful year they had been married, with a few that were beautiful but less blissful, and a tiny hourglass to indicate that he'd love her until the end of time. This was the most special and unique, knowing that it contained a part of her that he would take everywhere he went.

"I'm not leaving you anywhere. I know that you'll be with me forever," Lee whispered as he rubbed the charm and gathered his courage and composure. He was glad he was able to find a small space to himself on the bridge. There was no rush and no one to witness his struggle and release. "I love you, Iris. I'll love you forever. You deserve the world." With this last, shuddery declaration, he opened the urn and allowed a portion of Iris' ashes to flutter into the gentle waves of the Seine. This was his last place to visit; his last release.

After traveling to so many places that had been memorable and meaningful to them, and leaving a small part of Iris at each, he was finally ready to return home and allow himself to be enveloped in the loving hugs and care of his children, grandchildren, and loving family. He had finally kept his promise. He had given his beloved the world.

OBSESSION

*W*alking slowly in the shadows, I prayed he wouldn't notice me following him. Of course, he was with her. Rarely were they apart—he was always with her. Trying to find stolen moments where I could be with him alone was impossible. She smothered him; she was clingy, needy, and continuously watching him like a hawk.

It was clear to me that he could not relate to her. They were different in so many ways. Unsure if there was a connection between them, I wanted him so badly for myself. It seemed like they were always arguing. Witnessing her place her finger in his face, I wanted to take up for him, defend him, and rid him from her nagging ways. It upset me and I wanted to provide him solace in my personal care.

I hated her. She had everything I wished I had, and I was not above doing whatever it took to get everything I wanted, which included him. Spying from a distance, I watched him change out of his clothes. She was right there rubbing his back, smoothing his hair, poking, and prodding.

"Stop, stop it," I heard him say.

The behavior I witnessed her display was annoying as hell. He appeared like he didn't want to be bothered but forced himself to kiss her. She was the aggressor, and it angered me that she planted her lips on his beautiful, brown face. Her pale, pasty skin displayed no warmth; her skinny, boy-shaped body did not look like she could have handled him like I could.

My mind had me believing that I was a better fit for him, and I wanted him back. The problem was he was already in love with her, but I dreamt he would one day choose me. After all, he met me first. Our relationship was first. It was a deep bond that lasted close to a year. I was in love; I was obsessed. I fought hard to keep him, but ultimately, I lost. Now, he was with her, and I planned to do whatever I could to get him back into my life.

Watching him closely, I was looking for signs of happiness. It was a group date, and he was mostly conversing with his friends instead of her. I don't blame him I would ignore her too.

She paid for everything including the house they lived in and the clothes he wore. The fact that she did everything for him made it hard for me to compete. If I won him back, I would try to do all those things and more. I would travel to the moon and back to make sure his heart was all mine to assure he was happy. Running warm baths, placing the sweetest oils in the tub, rubbing his back after long days, massaging his feet, and soothing him until he was relaxed were all things I dreamt of doing for him. I would wash his clothes, adding extra fabric softener so that he smelled like sweet lavender every day.

Utilizing all my family recipes to cook all his favorite meals and make everything from scratch, would be the start to our own family tradition. Every day would be Christmas because I would give him tokens of my love every single chance I got.

Unsure if I could provide him with all the lavish things she provided him with, I wanted to make sure I did not buy his love. It was best if I earned it. I wanted it to be genuine, and I wanted him all for myself. Having him gaze into my eyes, and feel like we were all we needed, would be a win for me.

I decided to approach her while she watched him play ball. "Hello."

She looked me up and down and said a very dry, "Hi." Searching her face, I was not sure of what I was looking for. I felt things get awkward. She barked, "Can I help you with something?" I was heated she responded as if I did not belong there.

I wanted to say, "Bitch, can I help your ass with something? You are the third wheel." However, I played nice and spoke softly. "Oh, no. I thought you looked familiar. Who are you here with?"

"Number four is my guy." I pretended like I didn't know that already.

"Nice." I then lied. "Number eleven in the blue jersey is mine."

Forcing myself to make small talk just to see what I could pull out of her did not work. This woman was cold as ice with her eyes fixated on him. Pretending to leave something in my car, I walked away. I had to because I wanted to strangle her. Defeated, I went straight home.

"What happened? What's wrong?" he asked

"Nothing. You ready for dinner?" I tried to change the subject.

"You went to see him again, didn't you?"

I started crying and whispered, "Yes."

"Scarlett, this is becoming unhealthy. You are obsessed. I'm trying to be patient, but you're testing my love for you. This obsession is destroying our relationship!"

"Really? You're making this about you?"

"It's about us. We can't connect because you spend most of your time fantasizing about him."

Pondering my next words, I decided it was best to stay silent. Once I won the love of my life back, this fool would be dumped effective immediately.

The silence spoke volumes and upset him even more.

"You're checked out of this relationship, aren't you?"

Honesty won me over in that moment.

"I dunno. I am sorry, baby," I responded, whimpering.

Pain and anger came next, his words were fast and furious.

"If you were worthy of him, you would have him. I am tired of your ass tripping over something that you can no longer control. It's done. He's gone. Move on."

Wow. Those words cut me deep and had me stunned.

"You should be lucky she took his ass off you. Look at you. You're pitiful and would not have added any value to his life. Your family is piss poor thugs, and you're lucky that I took you in and wifed your ass," his rant continued.

Feeling stuck with a lump the size of an egg in my throat, I was frozen. It was partly out of fear of his wrath and partly because I placed myself in this position and had nobody to blame but myself.

Sean was a good husband. Graduating at the top of his class, with a master's degree in engineering from North Carolina A&T, he did well for himself. I had a law degree from North Carolina Central University, passed the bar, and never fulfilled my dream of opening my own law firm. Sean secured a job that moved us out of state, and I never got around to motivating myself enough to retake the bar exam. I got comfortable being a housewife, decorating my lavish home and catering to my husband's booming career and social circle.

Discovering more and more about myself as I spent a lot of time alone, I realized that I was not in love with my husband. It was a painful discovery because Sean was perfect—he just wasn't perfect for me. We had nothing in common. I thought his personality was dry. He made jokes all the time that were never funny, and he dressed in khakis and polo shirts and had zero swag.

What attracted me to him? I sat and often wondered.

I was broke, broken, and desperate for someone to accept me.

I got married at a young age before I really understood what I wanted in a man. I barely knew who I was as a young woman. Ten years later, I realized I was attracted to alpha males who were edgy. I loved men who worked with their hands and had an outgoing personality.

This got me into trouble, and Dillon was where I allowed my marriage to fall off track. Hiring a black contractor to renovate my home changed the trajectory of my life.

Bang!

Crash!

Buzz!

Clank!

Construction was in full swing in my home. Dillon was cool, making sure his employees were on task, securing permits, swinging a sledgehammer, and keeping me in the loop regarding my budget and timeline to completion. Dirty, wheat-colored Timberland boots, jeans, and a black company logoed t-shirt was his uniform. He wore a hard hat and sagged just enough to turn me on but not enough to see his drawers or catch a peek of his butt crack.

"Dillon, I ordered you guys several pizzas for lunch, and there is a cooler in the hall filled with cold, bottled water."

"You didn't have to do that, Mrs. Weddington."

"I know, but it's my pleasure. Just keep up the good work, and please call me Scarlett."

This was how it started.

Twenty-eight weeks later, I had a new kitchen, a new master bathroom, a fully renovated basement, and a romantic love affair with Dillon. Reflecting on what Dillon and I shared was so intense. It was taboo. It was divine. The chemistry I had with Dillon was magical. We laughed like we'd known each other for years. He was amazing at his job and explained things to me, which intrigued me and made me want to learn more about his profession.

A passionate lover with an appreciation of words was everything I wanted in my husband. Connecting on a level deeper than anything my marriage had ever seen caused me to consider walking away from Sean. Dillon talked about us starting a life together, having kids so that he could teach them the family business passing down his legacy. Falling in love with Dillon was inevitable.

"If I asked you to marry me, would you?" Dillon quizzed me.

"In a heartbeat, baby."

"You would give up all of this for me, Scarlett?"

"Absolutely. Why are you acting like you're surprised?"

"I dunno. I just cannot see myself without you, and it feels like I am being delusional to think this would work. I mean, you are married, baby."

"I know. It will work. It's not the ideal way to start a relationship, but sometimes things fall into place in unorthodox ways, and as long as we have love, we can make it work."

Dillon kissed me, and with his hand palming the side of my face, he looked me in my eyes and promised me a couple of forevers. We decided I would leave my husband to be with him.

Creeping up on the end of the project, my husband was pleased.

"How much longer, boss?" Sean said in the goofiest tone ever.

"Less than a week," Dillon responded in a voice that screamed, *I am six-foot-three, 220 pounds, and about to take your wife.*

"Good job! We are pleased with the work you guys have done here. It looks phenomenal. See you and the crew in the morning."

Walking away from their conversation, I was feeling nauseous. Watching my husband behave like a little kid on Christmas made me sick to my stomach. He had no fucking chill at all. He was giddy, excited, and practically drooling over Dillon because he was so satisfied with his work.

What a goofball, I thought to myself. I was eager to get this final week wrapped up so Dillon and I could put our plan in motion and start our life together.

Ring, ring.

"Hello," my husband answered. "WHAT? Awe, man! Okay, understood. Man, I hate to hear that. Okay. Do what you have to do. I understand. Okay, thanks for the call, man. My condolences."

"Who was that?" I questioned, drinking a glass of apple juice.

"Babe, that was Eric, Dillon's subcontractor. Dillon was killed in a car accident last night."

Crash!

Glass shattered all over my new ceramic tile floors, and apple juice splattered everywhere. Trying to run toward the sink, I didn't make it before vomiting all over, which caused me to slip and fall, cracking my head on the new floor.

"ARGGHHHHH!!!" Crying like a hysterical woman, I felt a sharp spear in my back from the shattered glass broken in the floor.

Waking up in the hospital, my husband was standing over me with concerned panic in his face.

"What happened? Where am I?" I sat up and looked around, confused.

Please, God, tell me I had a bad dream.

"Baby, you're in the hospital. You fell and cut your back up pretty bad," my husband explained while kissing me.

The door opened, and the doctor walked in.

"Mrs. Weddington, how are you feeling? You took a pretty hard fall there. We ran several tests, and the good news is that you're going to be fine. We got the glass out of your back and gave you a couple of stitches, and the best news is that your baby is fine, so please don't worry."

"Baby?" my husband said, baffled. My husband's loving concerned look quickly turned into anger. Sean suffered from azoospermia. He was unable to produce sperm; he realized my cries were because I was mourning the death of my lover.

Six years later, I still secretly mourned the death of Dillon. My life was hell, and I was more miserable than I had ever been with Sean. Unable to fully get over my affair, my husband took every available chance to verbally abuse me.

Mentally exhausted, emotionally drained, and financially dependent, I was in no shape to leave Sean. I would eventually, but until then, I would spend every single moment following and watching my son from afar while figuring out what I needed to do to reverse the adoption that Sean made me carry out.

SCHOOL DAYS

The shadows were getting long, telling me that it was getting late. We had planned to come up and work for an hour or two, but that had long expired. Even without looking at the clock, it was clear that evening was approaching. Just one more task. If I could accomplish one more thing, this classroom would look like a safe haven, an incubator for scholarships, the place where my students wanted and needed to be. The final touch was hanging the students' individual names on the door so they would know they belonged. With a triumphant "click," I hit the print button and sent the papers to be spit out of the ancient copy machine down the stairs and up the hall.

I started stacking and tidying, leaving nothing out but the tape needed to affix my students' names and cement this as their space. Just then a loud and unfamiliar, "HEY! STOP RIGHT

THERE!" Made me stop because I was not expecting a male's voice in the building.

I had heard my ten-year-old son's voice, still squeaky with youth, talking to another child, but we had no male teachers here, and from my experience, husbands didn't usually stick around to help with classroom setup once the heavy lifting was complete.

"What are you doing here?" I heard him shout.

At who? My son?

Before he could answer, the tall, blonde, burly man grabbed his arm, twisted it back, and pushed him roughly against the wall. The squeal of surprise and pain let me know that this bellow was directed at T. I still couldn't see what was happening, but I could hear the thud of my son's body and the clang of the lockers as they responded to his weight.

I raced out of the room, and toward the source of the commotion, now knowing that my son was involved. Faster than I had run in probably all of my combined adult years, I ensured that my voice arrived before my body. Whatever I had to do to put myself between my baby and this perceived danger.

"Wait! Stop! That's my son!"

"Mom," was all that he was able to get out of his mouth before the police officer shoved him to the ground.

"Stand right there, ma'am. Don't move." His voice was loud, deep, and demanding. Pausing momentarily, I looked back at my baby's face pushed into the tile floors. Looking at the tiles I so regularly heard the tap-tap of my heels from. Looking at the tiles I walked hand in hand with the babies of so many others. Tiles that now contained blood dripping from my child's nose. I ran toward him—how could I not?

"What is the problem? What are you doing to my son?"

"We've had some break-ins in the area. He definitely fits the description: young black boys, white t-shirts, basketball shorts, sneakers." He kneeled on my son's back even harder.

"What are you doing running around in here, huh? What are you trying to steal out of here and take to your little crew to sell?"

He asked these questions as though T had the oxygen available to speak. How could he speak when this full-grown man was kneeling directly on his back? T just gasped and cried.

The security officer then looked up at me. "And who are you? Are you with him?"

Far from my professional attire of knee length or lower dresses with sensible heels and perfectly coiffed hair, I was dressed in my weekend uniform of leggings, a tank top, and sneakers. My hair was in a loose afro. When I replied I was a teacher at the school, he didn't appear to believe me but at least leaned his weight on his other leg as he considered.

"Where's your ID, then?"

"My ID is upstairs in my classroom. Come with me, and I'll go get it."

Our moment of consideration seemed to expire as he frowned his face and laughed an ugly laugh. "Maybe a custodian or something. Ain't no colored teachers here."

Neither bothered nor surprised by the comment, but worried that this disgusting human would lean back onto my son and God knows what else, I took advantage of his shifted weight and lunged to grab T's arm to snatch him to me. The officer stepped back, and I thought we were about to be over this terrible ordeal; however, as my son started to stand and I raised my eyes, I saw that the officer had stepped back to give him room to unholster his weapon.

I put my hands in front of me and slung my son behind me. This situation had gone from irritating, to infuriating, to deadly all in the matter of moments. I knew beyond a shadow of a doubt that if my son was to get shot today, his would not be the first body to fall. I could feel him shaking. Terrified. His warm brown hand on my arm. This gave me courage to will my voice to stop trembling and calmly address this threat.

"Sir, my teacher's ID is right upstairs in my classroom. I am here working, and my son was just keeping me company."

"Nah, that's bullshit. Don't no colored teachers come around here. I used to go here myself."

"Can I please call my principal? She can tell you that we belong here!"

"Freeze! If you put your hands in your pockets, I'll put a bullet through you and that little brat."

It was surreal that even at the time with a gun pointing my way, my anger could overcome my fear. I had worked my way through school achieving a bachelor's and then master's degree. Highly qualified in my field, I had been hired to not only teach for a portion of the day but to provide a mentor and exemplar for my colleges as the campus' coach. Now, here he stood with his GED-appointed badge and weapon, threatening my child and insulting me?

His hand was still on the unholstered pistol when I raised my chin and stated, "I am going back to my classroom and taking my son with me. Expect to hear from your supervisor by Monday." I took another shaky breath and turned slightly to T and spoke only to him. "Come on. Let's get our things together and head home. I can finish this up on Monday, and I have some phone calls to make."

Looking braver than I actually felt, I gently pushed T ahead of me and turned my back to this man and put one foot in front of the other to walk up the stairs.

"Stop right there. Don't go another step," I could hear him say, now getting flustered and frustrated that the "coloreds" were not listening to and obeying him.

Careful to keep T in front of me, I raised my foot and walked up the next two steps, eyes on the top of the stairs, not even an inclination of turning to acknowledge this man.

The next three to five seconds happened so fast it was impossible to put the events in order. Everything seemed to happen at once. So many sounds, so much movement. There were two loud bangs. One was the sound of a heavy metal door being burst suddenly and enthusiastically opened; the other was the sound of a gun firing. Over all of this could be heard a joyful giggle and the impatient yell, "T, where are you? Where's the bouncy ball?" The next sounds were dull thuds and finally a scream. This scream was unlike any I had ever heard before, and it was coming from behind me.

"Maggggggiiiiieeeeeee!"

He ran past me with his arms now outstretched. As fast as things were moving just moments ago, now everything seemed in slow motion. The security guard ran up the four to five stairs to meet the body of the little girl with the Shirley Temple curls as she tumbled and then slid down. If you weren't close enough to see the nose and eyes that were almost mirror images of each other, you could tell by the way he was holding her so lovingly that she was very dear to him. As he screamed, the blood stain that bloomed with the commotion was now growing on her dress.

Without hesitation, I pulled my phone out of my pocket and called 9-1-1. After providing the necessary information, I sent T up to my classroom with the directions to close and lock the door, and I ran out to the front of the school to wave down the approaching ambulance.

The security guard kneeled with Maggie in his arms, apologizing over and over. "You scared me, big girl. I thought you were playing in my office. Please be ok," he kept begging. This sweet girl now looked confused, terrified, and in pain. Much like T had just moments ago.

Having been alerted by the security system, following close on the heels of the paramedics, was my principal. My face was the first she saw, and she immediately grabbed me up into a hug. "Kay, what on earth is going on here?"

The security guard glanced up momentarily to see us embrace as he was hustled away from his daughter so the paramedics could do their job. He looked at the floor, quickly realizing what I said was true and all that had come from his disbelief.

I heard one of the paramedics tell him, "She'll make it. Come and ride to the hospital with her." And he obediently followed. As he walked away, I could hear him telling the paramedic that he had just brought her in while he did a routine safety walk. I guess we had a lot more in common than he thought; we were both just trying to do the best we could at our jobs and as parents.

It was then the tears came. I sank down on the stairs, sobbing, allowing myself the release of tears for just a moment, then asked my principal to accompany me up to my classroom. I needed to see and be near my son, even before I could begin to explain what happened. When I walked in the door, we collapsed into each other's arms in an angry, sad, confused, frightened heap in the middle of these hallowed halls of learning.

MY BABY

We were having a screaming match, but I refused to back down. With balled fists and my anger rising, I was prepared to assassinate her with my words, destroying the friendship to the point of no return. She crossed the line. I would never be able to un-see what I saw, and I was not mature enough to accept her apology, forgive, nor move on. I had done that too many times to count.

She took her mammoth sized 11 foot, made contact, and kicked my baby! I couldn't understand how that was an accident. Especially when she snickered and said he fell backward *The Matrix* style. I grew more and more disgusted by her with each word she spewed, making light of the situation. I imagined punching her in the fucking nose when she smirked while reflecting on the incident.

I picked him up immediately to make sure he was ok.

"The little booger is fine. Stop tripping," she said.

It was futile constantly trying to make our friendship work. Kendall had so many great qualities; she was adventurous, spontaneous, smart, and focused. However, the shitty qualities were starting to overshadow the good ones. She was single, no kids, no husband, and had a great job making well over six figures. Kendall was one of the most selfish people I knew. She never had to share since she was an only child, and she was brought up in a home where her parents adorned her with everything she wanted. She rarely heard the word no.

Growing up, she was a true bitch. The uncanny beauty she was blessed with, along with her pampered and privileged childhood, made her feel like she was a princess. She was her parents' princess, but that title didn't cross over into my world. I still couldn't understand why I was so drawn to her. We were polar opposites.

As kids, it was rare to see a beautiful black family intact in my neighborhood. Unfortunately, most homes were made up of a mom, grandma, and children. Mine was made up of just my mother, my brother, and myself. Deep down, I was obsessed with her family unit. I was obsessed with her single-family, beautiful brick house and her parents, who appeared to be deeply in love. I wanted to be her. I thought she was so fortunate and had the world at her fingertips.

As adults, I realized her childhood contributed to a self-centered, conceited, entitled human product. I always thought she cared about me, proclaiming me her best friend, but that was a lie. I realized throughout childhood and college, I continually placed myself in unfavorable situations to help Kendall out. I wasn't sure she would do the same for me because when I got in a tight spot, she showed no interest or appeared to not have time.

The difference in our upbringings was me watching my mother finagle her way out of tight spots. Nothing came easy. Money was always tight. One income was all we had; she budgeted and taught us the difference between wants and needs at an early age. I never had anything to myself. I shared everything, including my room, food, clothes, time, and my space.

Kendall had it all, and she had it all to herself. The men were plentiful. The house was close to four thousand square feet. The job was top tier, and the wardrobe was top of the line. In comparison, I had a very different lifestyle. I had a life that was shared. I had a comfortable cozy home. My job paid well, my closet reflected good taste, and I only had one man, which was more than enough since he loved me enough to put a ring on it.

My baby was in my arms. Kendall had the audacity to say he was spoiled. I cut my eyes at her, daring her to say another word. It was in her best interest to pretend she was mute. The wrong word would've had my fist embedded into the walls of her skull.

While Kendall had been pregnant twice, she decided to abort both babies. Her parents forced her to get the first abortion because she was an 18-year-old college student pregnant by a frat boy. They expected her to graduate college and land a husband before becoming a mom. They threatened to cut off her finances, take her car, and stop paying her tuition, so she did as she was told. The second pregnancy was in her late twenties. She aborted this pregnancy because she was pregnant by a married man. Once he made it clear that a baby would never cause him to leave his family, she felt it was best to terminate the pregnancy and move on.

Motherhood was the elephant in the room when it came to our friendship. Kendall knew that I desperately wanted to give my husband a baby. I loved him so much I wanted to give him a baby. Unfortunately, we struggled conceiving for years. I was able to get pregnant, but I continuously miscarried.

It was the single most painful thing not being able to give birth. To not be able to give my husband a child. To not be able to fulfill the dream I had ever since I was a little girl to become a mommy. It tested my marriage and caused depression to sneak into my life. My faith in a higher power was questioned. Why me? When so many undeserving women like Kendall got pregnant and willingly aborted while women like me, who would give anything to experience motherhood, weren't successful in this area.

I was sensitive to the topic. Kendall and I never discussed her abortions. In return, I never bombarded her with my fertility issues, doctor's appointments, or maternal desires. It was another thing that strained our friendship because trying to conceive was such a massive part of my adult life.

Kendall could care less. She had no empathy, and since she was content with not experiencing the unconditional love of a child, she expected me to be content with that notion as well. I was not. She didn't even express over-the-moon happiness for me when I told her that I decided to adopt. That's when I knew it was time. This friendship has run its course, and I needed to stick a pin in it because it was done.

Motherhood was not a phase I was going through; it was something I desperately wanted to experience. I wanted to feel the connection of having a human growing inside of my body, attaching itself to me, needing me for everything in this world. The feeling of looking into the eyes of someone who shared my face, my bloodline, and own my heart is what I craved in order to feel whole. Adopting my baby wasn't quite the same. However, I believed it saved my marriage and eased my heartache by giving me something to care for and pour my love into making life for me complete.

I took the baby upstairs and came back down to end this thing with Kendall. She was relaxing in my den, drinking bottled water with her legs crossed as if a major fight didn't transpire. I slapped her on her leg, shouting, "Leave. Just go! We're done!"

"What? Stop being dramatic, whatever."

"I'm not playing, Kendall. This right here between us no longer makes me happy. When I am with you, it should be easy and fun, not exhausting and stressful."

She stood up and looked at me with her head cocked sideways.

"Get out of my house, Kendall. I need to clear my mental headspace, tidy up, and get dinner started before Trace gets home from work," I said.

While I gathered her Gucci bag and keys to hand her, I felt a push. *Whap!* I fell backward onto the sectional. Kendall threw her last swallow of water on my crouch and then dove head first in between my legs, moving my now soaked panties to the side wildly, kissing and sucking on my lower lips.

"Mmmmnnn," I moaned.

I unbuttoned my shirt dress, giving her access to my breasts. As my river started to flow, Kendall leaned up, slipped my panties off, and removed her jersey-knit dress. She grabbed my ankle and placed me in the scissor position, frantically moving north and south on my mound. I was in heaven. Kendall brought my ankle to her mouth and licked the bottom of my foot; the warm wet sensation sent shivers through my body. I gripped her waist, forcing rapid back and forth movements from her hips until I climaxed.

Kendell leaned over, kissed my mouth, and looked at me.

"You always taste so good," she told me.

I couldn't speak. I was breathing heavily. I smiled.

"You ain't never getting rid of me! You better be glad I allow my pussy to be shared with Trace." I kissed her back and squeezed her perfect 38 D-cup breasts.

"Get your ass up for real now and go. I have to get cleaned up and get dinner going."

Muah Muah Muah. Three more kisses to my lady parts, and Kendall got up from on top of me to prepare to leave.

My baby came running downstairs. I guess all the noise Kendell and I made startled him. His tail was wagging as he jumped on the couch and licked my face.

Kendall patted his head and smiled

"See, your spoiled ass fur baby is fine."

UP THE COAST I

*T*he first words I said this morning were happy anniversary. As I smiled into my beloved's face and kissed her gently awake, I could feel the familiar stone in my heart. This heaviness was not getting easier to bear, but this was definitely not the day to relieve it.

My curves slid in closer next to hers and she sleepily looked at my face while simultaneously pulling me in closer. As we laid face to face, chest to chest, torso to torso, thigh to thigh, all I could think about was, *damn, we fit just right.* It seemed like our curves were made in the yin and yang symbol, destined to adhere to each other, mystical, magnetic, adhesive. This was not the only fit. Our bodies aligned perfectly, but so did the rest. Her calm and quiet to my explosive. Her artistic to my focused logic. I loved how she appreciated and complemented everything about who I am.

I continued to murmur happy anniversary and sweet nothings into her beautiful, patchouli scented locs. Although our love was still new, she was familiar to me. Her almond brown skin contrasted against my mahogany skin. As her eyes opened sleepily, I stared into them, having already memorized every color, fleck, and curve, she mirrored my gaze. I could see myself in her eyes, literally and figuratively. Her naturally long and upturned lashes, a style that women were paying routinely for, added to her look of innocence. As we made celebratory love to commemorate the 365 days since our first official date and the 182 days since we had signed a lease. I pushed back all thoughts of the pain I had the potential to cause her and poured my all into pleasing her right now.

***

"I wish you didn't have to go into work this week. Don't you think you can get a few extra days? It is our anniversary..."

Okoye turned from the stove and looked me directly in my eyes. It was clear she was trying to decide whether to try beguiling or arguing. We had this conversation almost weekly. My stomach was a little aflutter, but I knew how this would go.

"Now you know they not gon' let me bring home all these coins and not put in the work." I slid in and wrapped my arms around her as she plated our Sunday brunch. The plate she set down in front of me arranged as though Matisse himself had touched it. Fluffy scrambled eggs, plump shrimp, both sauteed and fried, crispy bacon, creamy grits, and delicious little pastries.

She mumbled a grudging acknowledgment and then sat down beside me to enjoy the food. This was always the hardest part of the weekend. We both knew I had to leave soon; however, we both had very much different understandings of why I was leaving. Her understanding of my position was based on carefully crafted lies. Lies I used to protect her heart even though I knew they had the potential to shatter it.

With my job as an insurance adjuster, it was not at all uncommon for my assignments to take me to different cities and cause extended stays away depending on the length and nature of my assignment. When we first started seeing each other, I was mostly honest about my work. Okoye knew I was an insurance adjuster. She knew I worked in DC Monday through Friday 16-hour days. She knew I brought home more than enough money to pay the rent on our top-floor apartment with a view of the Miami skyline. She knew I maintained an apartment in DC nearby to the office to sleep and live when I had to be far away from her, and she knew that I did not live alone.

Six months ago, when she had been stressed and distracted on one too many of my visits or homecoming (whatever you want to call it) that her art was selling too inconsistently for her financial comfort, on our next weekend together she was presented with a key to 'our place.' I could afford it, and I was happy to provide that level of security for her, for us. Our following date was a trip to far too many furniture stores and decorator outlets as we made this place feel like a home. Like our home. I would have never thought I would make a home with another woman as my partner. Simply put, I loved her.

I remembered our unlikely start. I had acclimated easily to life at University of Miami. They had everything on my college agenda. With my son's father holding up his end of the bargain, and my aunt's help and support, I was able to get out and about and move around easily. I loved my son dearly and was the best mother I could be, but I was also 19 and eager to act every bit of my age.

Even though I was living my party girl dreams, I was still taking care of business on the academic and business fronts as well. By my senior year, I was serving on the recruitment and retention student board at the university. This involved me going on home visits with university staff, helping them convince students and their families to come to our school, and then making sure they are doing well and successful and able to stay through graduation. It was part of my job to smile at nervous tentative freshmen and assure parents I would make sure they didn't pass out drunk on a fraternity house floor within the first few weeks of school. My record was almost perfect.

I'll never forget when I met Okoye. She was quiet as a church mouse, even in her own house. She was kind and friendly, but I could tell there was so much more under the surface. As my staff counterpart spoke with her parents in the living room, she invited me to walk to the kitchen with her to help her get drinks for everyone. Once we were in the kitchen, she poured tall glasses of Minute Maid for everyone, then she poured a shooter of gin straight into hers and then offered me one for my glass.

By this point, I had almost completed my bucket list of college antics, but I would make an exception for just one more if this young, innocent girl decided to listen to our advice. Okoye enrolled at U of M as a fine arts major, and I did all I could to help her get acclimated. We maintained a friendship, I was super busy with my duties as mom, student, board member, and party girl. We were able to sneak in a few lunches and brunches, but she was not into the party scene, and I was trying to make the most of the few months of college I had remaining before I had to become a "real adult." I attended as many of her shows as possible; her full and melodic voice vibrated through my very essence each time I heard it.

The night before graduation, just a few days before I was set to leave, I heard an unexpected knock. I opened the door to find Okoye standing there with a bottle of gin, the same kind as the shooter she had at our first meeting.

"I wanted to say goodbye and maybe celebrate with you a little before you leave. You were the main reason that I ended up here at U of M, and I never got to properly thank you."

I welcomed her in. I grabbed two glasses and the carton of Minute Maid. I noticed instead of shooters of gin, she had graduated up to a pint. My aunt and son, Zay, had gone to spend the night at the hotel with the family that had gathered in town, allegedly for my graduation, but I think the beautiful beaches of Miami were a motivator as well. I had decided to stay at the house for one last night, reflecting on all that changed.

Okoye sat on the couch and drank and reminisced about all we encountered in her first year and my last. I felt warm from the inside from the liquor, and I could see her face was flushed too. The conversation hit a brief lull; it was a comfortable silence. I could tell it was laced with more than the smell of the incense I had lit and the blunt we passed back and forth.

Before I knew it, her mouth was wet and hot on mine. All shyness was out the window. She firmly, yet gently, pushed me into a reclining position on the couch and covered every exposed area with kisses. Then, insistently, Okoye pulled up my shirt and exposed my breasts, unbridled by a bra in my nightclothes after just stepping out of the shower. I was shocked but open to whatever may happen. Her kisses and the gin had my mind swirling. I led her to the bedroom that I would be living in for one last night. We made love like there had never been another for either of us. I rounded out my list of firsts during my matriculation at the University of Miami.

At my graduation the next day, Okoye brought me a bouquet of flowers and hugged me as though nothing had happened. I went on to my position in DC, and we kept in touch somewhat, but not consistently.

Finally, years later, on a trip to Miami to visit with my aunt, as we enjoyed a cocktail in one of the local venues, I heard a voice I hadn't heard in ages. Before the next line could hit my ears, I knew it was Okoye performing on the stage. I walked to the edge of the stage so that my face was the first she saw when she completed her number and exited. Our eyes locked, and she paused a moment before she left the stage. She didn't leave my arms for the rest of the weekend.

Now, over a year later, I stood before her tear-stained face as she watched me pack up my bags. It was harder and harder to break her heart with every visit. We got into a brief war of words, then repeat it, then yelled the necessity for me to get on the plane.

Pretending it was anger but truly propelled by guilt, I walked out the door and towards the car. I hesitated at the car door, just as my phone chimed. All flights out of MIA were canceled until 6 a.m. due to the weather.

I looked up at the picture window to see Okoye looking down at me. As I walked into the house, I surreptitiously deleted the weather text from the airline after I quickly took a screenshot and sent it with a sad face with a message saying, see you in the morning with a sad face.

Walking back up the walkway and into Okoye's arms, I held her and told her I was just going to spend the night and head back in the morning. I let her believe I couldn't bear to leave her, and while it was true I'd enjoy the extra hours of quality time, I knew there would be hell to pay on the other end.

Passion

THE DATE

He had all the features that made me swoon. This man was blessed with beautiful deep dimples, and his legs were slightly bowed. I visualized his manhood was so thick and long that it literally hammered his legs, bending them ever so slightly into the bowlegs he had. This black king had smooth caramel skin, the kind of skin that looked healthy, hydrated, and moisturized and was medium build, and I could tell that he had a relationship with a gym.

His hands were smooth, nails were clean and buffed and his hands were without callouses. I wondered if he ever did any manual labor. If he could change a tire? Putty a wall? None of that really mattered because his income allowed him to outsource any of those tasks if he wanted to. He walked like a Zulu warrior: confident, highly skilled, with a hint of danger to his stride. I loved that he was confident and assured me in so many words that he would slay the task at hand. Looking at the sincerity in his eyes I had no doubts that he was more than capable of making me extremely happy.

When he turned to walk into the other room, I watched him until he faded behind the door. His long locs were pulled back into a neat ponytail and gently swayed left to right with each step. The tips were colored light brown, and they hit the middle of his back. I wondered if his hair was heavy. Did he mind them being grabbed or pulled? Or was he like so many of us who said, "Nah, don't touch my hair?"

I noticed how thick and healthy they were and wondered if he would let me massage, wash, and re-twist his hair. It would be a labor of love, and I would be honored to help support his natural hair journey. He had a lineup that was perfection, his chin showcased a thick, well-trimmed beard with thin sideburns that ran up into his locs. His mustache sat on a perfect set of pink full lips. I visualized myself sucking them, gently biting them, and softly tugging on his lower lip.

It was our first time with each other, so I wasn't sure what to expect. I was extremely nervous. My stomach was churning, gut bubbling, and suddenly, my stomach was filled with gas. I refused to let it slip because every time I thought I could sneak and release a silent one, it came out loud and explosive. I couldn't let him experience me in that way. We didn't know each other like that yet.

His cologne was a nice and clean earthy scent. I hoped it would last and linger for the duration of our experience, although there would be a chance he would be sweaty afterward. That didn't matter to me. I fully anticipated for him to put in some serious work and I knew that I'd be a challenge for him. My expectation was to be pleased. I waited a long time, and I was more than ready.

We met about six months ago. Although he expressed he wanted to "do it" back then, I felt it was best if we waited. Honestly, I wasn't mentally there at that time. Nervous energy washed over me; I wanted to make sure that I was prepared for this invaluable experience. The baritone in his voice almost made me do it immediately. When he spoke I melted, got lost in his words, and had no idea what he was saying since I was too busy soothing my soul with his voice.

One time, during one of our initial conversations, he said, "How do you feel about that?" "huh?" I questioned. Poor thing had to repeat the whole entire conversation because I was dreaming with my eyes open. He was such a teddy bear, repeating himself, I tried hard to stay focused the next time around.

Another time, he leaned in and placed his hands around my face. He then slid his finger in my mouth. I thought, *Oh, wow! It's happening.* I was trying to think quick. *Should I suck his finger? Should I move it in and out provocatively like they did in pornographic movies?* I must have thought too long, because before I could make a move, his hand was out. Damn! I missed my chance, and now the moment had passed.

I was too embarrassed to say, "Wait! Wait a second, honey. Place your finger back in there. My mouth is moist and wet and ready to slob on your finger. I'm ready now!" Well . . . not only did I miss the moment, but before I realized what was happening, he was wiping my face. I had slob running down my damn chin. Shit! How fucking unsexy was that? This fine ass dude was wiping spit from my face. He then handed me a warm cloth. I was mortified.

He smiled and said, "No worries. It happens."

Talk about awkward.

As he began, he told me to try and relax. He tried to make me feel at ease by telling me that I was in good hands . . . those hands . . . they were the perfect size to enclose my boobs. When he leaned in, I inhaled deeply, taking in his scent. I noticed he was wearing a thick figaro gold chain with a cross attached. It was a modest chain, and I wondered how strong it was. Would it snap easily in the throes of passion? Would he forgive me if I popped it?

He said, "I am going to lay you down now."

"Dude, throw my ass down! Push me down! Shit, body slam my ass down and force me to lay back, just have your way!" is how I wanted to respond, But he was sweet and behaving like a gentleman, and I went with the flow so I could fully embrace the experience and not expose my thirsty ways.

Looking over, he had a table set up with several odd items on them. I was taken aback. *Damn . . . he's a freak!* I thought to myself.

"Are you going to be using all of those on me?" I asked sheepishly.

He turned back and looked at his gadgets then smiled, "Yep. Don't let them scare you. They will help me get the job done. I will be gentle. My number-one goal is to make sure you're completely satisfied."

"Okay. I completely trust you." I responded smiling like a young schoolgirl, That was true. I felt so comfortable with this beautiful black man and trusted him, and instinctually, knew that he would take good care of me.

I was ready, wearing a very comfortable long maxi dress with sandals. My pedicure was fresh, and my toes were painted white. That was my favorite color against my milk chocolate skin. I had on my matching Love Vera panty set. It was an emerald-green cage cut-out bra with delicate lace along with a triple-strapped thong. I felt so feminine and sexy under my outfit, and I longed for him to run his hands up my dress, slide my panties to the side, and have his way with my nether regions.

Before I knew it, he gazed deeply into my eyes, smiling, "How was that?" He asked

"How was what?" baffled and blinking several times I did not feel a thing. There was no way he was finished. Dude looked like he was packing heat! I knew for sure he was. While I never saw the actual snake, I saw the imprint and once felt it brush ever so slightly against my arm one time when we were together. I was laid back on his massive leather chair that reclined into a straight horizontal position. He stood up slowly and stood over me and I saw it gathered, then I watched it drop. There was no way I didn't feel anything.

"That's what good drugs will do to you." When he said that I paused in disbelief.

I gasped. Did this fool drug me? Was this a damn joke? He smiled at me like this was a damn joke! I had never taken drugs in my life, never even smoked weed. I barely drank alcohol, and when I did it was so that I can be social. Even then, I nursed a drink the entire night. Unable to believe that he drugged me, then he smiled like it was okay! Instantly I went from adoring him to realizing that I was about to catch a homicide case over his ass! He did not have to drug me. My ass was down with whatever from the jump!

My eyes fluttered, and I was at a loss for words. I then, with tears forming in my eyes, said, "Why did you feel the need to drug me?"

He looked at me like I was a unicorn, "Huh?"

"You heard me. Why did you feel the need to drug me?" Breathing heavy I repeated myself.

"Did you expect me to remove four impacted wisdom teeth without providing you with a mild sedation?" He asked frowning.

I sat straight up and looked around . . . at that moment, that fart I tried so hard to hold on to escaped.

CALLER ARE YOU THERE?

"*I*'m not even about to tell you how they had me fucked up in here today! You won't even believe it. Don't worry, I got it straightened out, though!"

"Yeah, I know, Thugzilla. I worry more about them. I know you can hold your own."

These words of confidence from my adoring husband, plus his velvety voice, never failed to bring a smile to my face. I was grinning from ear to ear now, despite sitting at my desk on a Monday morning, already irritated by my co-workers.

"My beautiful, sexy, intelligent, powerful . . ."

"Go on, go on."

". . . ambitious, sensual, captivating . . ."

"Ok, ok!"

". . . wife. I miss you already."

"I should be home at the regular time. I miss you. I'm cutting out

ASAP."

"You don't miss me. If you missed me, you'd be right here in my arms right now."

"Oh, really? Do tell." I loved when our conversations got flirty. After all these years of marriage, this man still turned me on so much.

"You don't miss me because if you missed me, my arms would be wrapped around you, squeezing you close."

"You don't say," I purred into the phone. "What else?"

"Well, you know I love feeling your body on mine, especially when you sleep naked. As I squeeze you close to me . . . my hands. I probably wouldn't be able to help myself. They'd start roaming."

"Oh, really? Where?" I asked.

"All over. One hand would probably slide down and rub the curve of your hip and cup it around back up your ass cheek. He'd probably have to hang out there a minute. Give it a little squeeze action. You know that's one of my favorite features."

"Is that right?" I responded in almost a whisper.

"Absolutely. Then, I would probably let that hand slide back up to your waist and trace that curve again. I love that dip down for your waist and how smooth and round it arcs back up to your hip. It's like a Van Gogh, baby."

"Marvelous taste in art—"

"Um, excuse me, Mrs. Washington. I did knock," my project manager said as she rudely walked into my office.

My mind said, *did you hear me say come in? Rude ass heffa!* But my mouth, which enjoyed the privilege of eating through my employment, said, "I didn't hear you, but anyhow, I'm just wrapping up here. I'll be right with you."

I directed my attention back to my husband, who had momentarily paused when he heard that we were interrupted.

"You had mentioned some artwork?" My side of the conversation was completely innocent. Every response I gave him was ambiguous due to my presence at work. At our design firm, nothing I said would be taken as a personal call, much less a sexy, personal call. He didn't mind my lack of specificity, he knew the effect he had on me, and he enjoyed knowing that he could talk as freaky to me as he wanted, and I could not respond in kind.

"That other hand, though, I think he'd slide up."

"Where again?"

"He would definitely slide up your stomach."

"No, skip that part. I'm not fond of the curves and lines there," I said with an ironic chuckle. I hated my pudgy stomach, full of stretch marks.

"He wouldn't dare. That part carried my babies safe and sound and changed for their every need to finally bring them into the world. I would spend a little extra time there too. Follow every line and curve and personally thank each and every one for being a part of you."

"You certainly have interesting tastes, sir." Remember what I said before about the voice, the words? I was beaming once again. I looked up with my huge smile, and to my surprise, my boss was still standing in my doorway. She was now smiling at me.

My smile turned to a look of confusion. I meant my statement as a dismissal, but apparently, she took it as an invitation to stand and wait.

"Umm," I started into the phone just as I heard a small deep laugh come from my sexy hubby.

"Nah, I got your attention now, lady. Get rid of her. I'm going to keep telling you about those hands."

"Mrs. Washington, I just wanted to give you a couple of client contacts. They need to be finalized by the end of the week and may need you to reach out to confirm information."

"Thank you. Can you put them on here, please?" I asked, handing her a pen and pad of sticky notes. She walked closer to my desk to write the numbers on the paper.

"So, that other hand, after it paid its gratitude, would probably keep sliding up and cup one of those pretty titties."

This time, I didn't say anything in reply. I didn't trust myself.

"Shoot! I thought I had it pulled up. Hold on," said the voice in front of me, now scrolling on her phone. She could have did that shit in her own office!

"And depending on how many times I had rode that roller coaster curve of her thigh to hip to slim waistline to bust with my other hand, he might have to pinch that nipple with his first finger and thumb. I know that's gon' make you arch that back and push that ass up on me."

I started squirming in my seat a little as I felt my flower starting to blossom and wished that Jane would hurry up and get out of my office.

"There it is!" she exclaimed and picked up the pen. *Hurry up!*

"I, um . . ." My witty quips were not able to tear my focus away from the velvet massaging in my ear, and I was unable to get this distraction out of my office. "Ok, well, thanks!" I said to Jane again, attempting to dismiss her.

She put the pen down on my desk and turned to go but stopped just a few feet away. Meanwhile, my hubby continued what he had started.

"When you push that ass back on me, it feels so good that I'd probably have to roll us both over on our backs—you right on top of me. I want to feel the weight of your body pressing down on me. Feel your skin on me from your heels to the top of your head, rub and squeeze all over your body."

"By the way, did you get a chance to transfer those files to the removable drive? Did you have it with you today?"

"Hm, um, y-yes. Just one second." Some people were not raised with any manners whatsoever. I knew she could see that I was still on the phone. Yes, I was technically having phone sex at my desk, but she didn't know who I was talking to! I reached down into the drawer to grab my work bag as I continued to listen to my phone call.

"You still there, baby?" he asked. I knew he could hear Jane's voice close to me and that he was enjoying every minute of this sweet torture.

"Mm hmm."

"When you lay on top of me like that, you can feel how hard just touching you makes me. By this time, I'm going to be ready to spread my legs and hope you'll do the same on top of me so I can squeeze those thighs and touch that ocean in between. When you start arching your back even more . . . mm mm mm!"

I rummaged through my bag, searching for the zip drive and hopefully the key to getting this heffa out of my office so I could have a private word with my husband.

"When you arch that back again, I would grab you around your waist and move your hips like they were a game controller. I'd put you in perfect position to slide right inside you." He made a noise somewhere between a moan and a gasp that let me know that he was wishing I was there just as much as I was. "Then, you would probably sit straight up and sit on me, pushing me deeper. That's what you would do if you missed me."

I sighed from both desire and relief when I found the zip drive and quickly handed it to Jane. "Don't forget about Judy's birthday luncheon today!" she said as she turned to walk out of my office.

"Sorry, I have to go home for lunch. I forgot some materials that I need later."

"Oh, that's a shame. Well, I'll let her know." Jane stopped at the door and turned to face me once again before leaving. "And, Mrs. Washington, you might want to turn the volume down on your phone. We wouldn't want to compromise any confidential client information, would we?" She didn't wait for my answer, just gave me a small smile, and walked down the hall.

FAMILY UNIT

I cried on Maverick's shoulder for the umpteenth time this week. I was extremely emotional and unable to control my outburst. Realizing I was in a state of shock to learn my husband, who I always thought was the best man I ever encountered, was cheating on me.

Months ago, I noticed little things that gave me red flags because things were outside of the norm. My husband was a traditional guy. He had a routine, and rarely did he stray from it.

It started with me dropping by his office. He was out to lunch, and that was weird because my husband never left for lunch. I assumed he wanted a change of scenery, forgot to take his lunch, or simply didn't want the food in the cafeteria, and decided to go out. It was a beautiful fall day. It was out of the norm but not weird.

Then he started having weekend appointments and began catching up with paperwork on the weekends. My husband worked a lot. He managed close to 150 employees, and sometimes he worked on Saturday mornings. Most often, he worked in our home office, so him going into the office was different.

The moment that had me feeling something was off was when I was coming in from the grocery store and passed my husband coming into our neighborhood. He was coming from the opposite direction of his job. I asked him about it, and he simply said, "I took a different route."

"Huh?" I questioned. "What different route?"

"I wanted to try some back roads."

Up to that point, Anthony had been on his job for 16 years. What different route magically appeared after all this time? There was no new construction, no new highways, so that was weird to me.

"Oh okay," I stated, making a mental note in the back of my mind.

It bothered me, so I called Maverick. My husband and Maverick were close, and I adored him. He was slightly older than my husband; he was a great role model for him. Ten years his senior, Maverick always provided my husband with great advice. Maverick was my husband's go-to, and he soon became mine as well.

Maverick was what I considered a cat daddy. He was smooth, well dressed, and knew what to say and when to say it.

Twice divorced, he often gave us advice on the marriage pitfalls to avoid and how to stay connected in our union. He shared things that he wished he knew before committing.

In the beginning, I felt weird for going to Maverick with my concerns. I was comforted by his words, and he assured me that my husband was faithful.

"Would you tell me if Anthony was cheating on me?" I asked.

"Would you want me to tell you? Honestly? Could you handle that?"

Not knowing how to respond, I wasn't sure if I was ready to hear confirmation he was cheating. I now wondered if Maverick knew something and wasn't telling me.

"Reagan, sometimes things are complicated. Men can have sex with another female, but that does not mean that they don't love their wives. Sometimes it is just purely physical."

I broke down. "Did you just confirm that he's having an affair?"

"See, this is why I hate to be involved. I feel horrible. I followed him like you asked, and I snapped some pictures. I did see him with someone, and unfortunately, it was your cousin."

"What? Are you fucking serious?"

Walking across my den to join me on the love seat, Maverick then showed me some pictures. My husband was smiling and laughing with my cousin in the corner of a dimly lit restaurant. My heart was beating so rapidly I thought it would burst.

"Reagan, don't jump to conclusions; it could be innocent."

"That's my first cousin! We are close, and she's been in my home and stayed over tons of times. I don't think she would do that to me. Maybe they were just having an innocent lunch."

"Maybe," Maverick said, throwing both arms up. "I felt the same way…. until," he didn't finish.

"Until what?"

Silence

"Until what, Maverick!"

Sighing deeply, he continued.

"Until I kept following him and saw this."

He proceeded to show me pictures from the prior week of them walking into a hotel. Maverick showed me several pictures on separate days of them walking in or out of different hotels. The pictures were during times my husband told me that he was working late or catching up on paperwork during the weekend.

"Reagan, I am not sure what to think. I love Ant, but these photos are a little suspicious," Maverick whispered in a solemn tone.

"Arghhhh," I went into a rage.

Maverick hugged me hard.

"Reagan, I am so sorry. I hate to be the one to break this news to you. I love you, and I hate to see you hurting like this."

Maverick looked me in my eye. "Have I ever given you or Ant bad advice?" I looked into his eyes and said *no* in between sobs. "Well, listen to me. You have a great life with Anthony. He may be going through a brief midlife crisis."

Heartbroken, I whispered, "Cheating may have been forgivable, but cheating with my cousin is a deal-breaker."

Maverick held me by my shoulders.

"Do you think I am a bad person?"

"Of course not," I told him.

"I've been a victim of making bad choices, but I learned from them, and I grew from them. They don't make me a bad person. Anthony is not a bad person, and neither are you. It's okay if you decide to forgive him. People make mistakes."

I agreed. "I don't think I can get over this, Maverick."

"What would make you feel better. Do you want to dissolve your marriage? Start from scratch? Find a job to maintain your lifestyle? Give up your help, your vacation home? What type of man are you going to find that you can trust, loves you genuinely, and not just want you because of what you already have? It's tough out here, Reagan. Just think about everything from all perspectives before you make a move."

"Shit!" I screamed. I did have a lot to think about. "I don't see myself turning a blind eye, Maverick. The only thing that would make me feel better is revenge. Getting me a side piece."

Maverick slapped his palms together. "Whatever you do, make sure the person has as much to lose as you do, be discreet because men don't forgive as easily as women do. I know it's a double standard, but it's the truth," he warned.

After conversing for hours with Maverick, he helped me cope better. Being vulnerable and comforted by Maverick felt natural. I was faced with some hard decisions but talking through all of my what-ifs made me feel less alone. He quickly became my confidant, and before I knew it, my lover.

When having that conversation with Maverick, I didn't anticipate he would turn into my side piece. Being with him was explosive. He was a better, more experienced, refined version of my husband. I could not get enough of his loving. My husband's lies, and sudden excuses to leave for hours, gave me ample opportunity to get it in with Maverick.

One day, after an intense romp in my bed, Maverick said, "Reagan, how did we get to this point? Don't you think we should cool it? This shit feels dirty."

"I thought you told me you like it dirty."

Maverick smiled. His salt and pepper beard were giving him a distinguished sexy look. I stood up in front of him. He turned me around and playfully bit me on my ass cheek.

"We have to stop this. The guilt is getting to me."

"I don't feel guilty at all. You have helped me cope these past couple of months, and you make me feel good."

My husband decided to cheat at the worst time. I was reaching my sexual peak, and Maverick was benefiting from all this good loving. I decided I was leaving Anthony. I did not realize what I was missing until I started sleeping with Maverick. The sex was wild, exciting, and I could not get enough of this man. I thought about him every day, all day.

It was becoming harder and harder to be with my husband. I just laid there oohing and aahhhing until it was done. I was tired of performing. I wanted out.

It was my birthday, but I did not want to celebrate it. I certainly did not want to celebrate with my husband. He was lucky my ass was still around. I had been going through the motions for the past three months while plotting and planning my escape. Assuring that I had enough money tucked away to start over after I left him was the only thing that kept me on his arm. It pissed me off how he was living a double life, sneaking away to see her while coming home happy, like the perfect husband to me.

"Be careful, baby."

I guess he felt I couldn't walk in 4-inch heels. I never needed his help before, so why he felt the need to help me now was beyond me. I assumed now that he was sleeping with a 24-year-old, me turning 40 was geriatric, and I needed help walking. I didn't even want to go to dinner with him. It was a struggle dealing with him lately. I wasn't made for acting.

"Lying cheating ass bastard," I whispered under my breath.

"I got it. I see the cracked pavement. I'm good." I pulled away.

He was smiling like a Cheshire cat. I looked at him and wondered to myself, *who did I marry?*

"Baby, you look absolutely stunning tonight."

"Thanks," I gave him a lackluster response.

Oblivious to my underwhelming birthday attitude, he grabbed my hand and walked me into the Umstead Hotel. I always wanted to have dinner here, but I wondered in the back of my head if he had taken her here. Did they have one of their many trysts in this same hotel?

"I know you always wanted to dine here, so I thought it would be special to have dinner here for your birthday," he said, snapping me out of my trance. I gave him a weak smile.

Placing his hand on the small of my back, the hostess walked us to our reserved space. I quickened my pace behind the hostess to try and remove his hand from my body. He was on this ass, so that didn't work. The hostess opened the doors, and before I fully stepped into the room, I was met with…

"Surprise!" Blinking rapidly, I was overwhelmed with the sea of people in front of me. There were friends and family members, both local and from out of state. There were balloons and fresh flowers all over the room. I saw a massive hologram saying: **Reagan's Fabulous at 40 Birthday Bash**, high up on the back wall. People were hugging and kissing me. My mom was there! I hadn't seen her in almost a year. My nephew, who went to school in California, and so many of my loved ones were present.

Tears started flowing. I couldn't speak. A beautiful 4-tiered cake was posted up in the corner.

My husband grabbed the mic.

"I think I got her, fam! My baby is truly surprised, which is hard to do. I must take a moment to say welcome, enjoy yourself, eat, drink, and dance all night long. We want to make this a memorable night for my queen. She is truly 40 and fabulous."

Lifting my hand and kissing it, he continued. "I also want to thank her favorite cousin, Micah, who was extremely instrumental in helping me with all the details, décor, and party planning needed to pull this surprise off for the love of my life. I also want to thank my favorite uncle, Rick, who is more like my brother since he is only 10 years older than me and my mom practically raised us together, he was instrumental in helping me keep my wife distracted while handling the logistics of getting family settled with flights and hotels. It was hard containing this for the last couple of months, but we did it, guys. We got her good!"

My face instantly felt flush like some lit a match in my insides. Looking over in his Uncle Maverick's direction, he was standing at one of the many cocktail tables with a drink in his hand. He raised his glass, winked at me, and walked over to the dance floor, and started dancing.

"Baby… Baby…You haven't said anything. Are you in shock?" My husband was grinning hard, showing all his beautifully aligned teeth.

I suddenly felt sick. I looked at his handsome, innocent face, and before I could respond, I passed out.

ON THE ROAD

The sun was slipping down the horizon, unfortunately, she was not sliding down the highway as she had hoped. What a day. This Friday evening was well deserved after the week she'd had . . . if only she could get to her hot date.

Her daily grind included crunching numbers behind a desk, using her customer service voice, and using every spare minute she could to build her health and wellness business. She was ready to get out of her car and step over every mile of traffic like a giant so that she could quickly get to her destination. Despite being alone in the car, she cursed out loud. "Fuuuuuuck!" She knew her rush to get home was futile, so she unbuckled her seatbelt and settled with stepping out of her car to stretch. Along with other drivers in the area, she craned her neck to see if things were moving forward. But beyond the sea of stopped cars, she could see only flashing lights, red and blue lights of different heights in the distance.

"For all I know, it could be an accident or road construction that was keeping me from my destination," she muttered. She reached above her head and swayed her slim, thick body from side to side, her stiff body getting just a little relief from the stiffness that threatened to creep in from sitting in one position too long. Position . . . COME ON, TRAFFIC! This time, not aloud, but equally as heartfelt.

It was date night. She needed to get home and get ready!

She walked a few car lengths, trying to see more, sneaky side glances at the cars near her. Carloads of young people, too many in the car, too many distractions. This traffic was probably a good thing, slow them down a little. Her next thought, *Girl, when did you get so old? Let the kids enjoy themselves . . . safely, of course.*

The next car was an older lady driving alone with a few paper bags of groceries. She was probably worrying about getting her milk and ice cream home and in the cold. *I know it's butter pecan. She's definitely in the butter pecan demographic,* she thought to herself.

She turned her neck up a few extra degrees to peek in the mirror at the eighteen-wheeler to the right. She had noticed him pulling up even before traffic ground to a complete halt and wondered if he would be able to maneuver that big old thang through traffic. He seemed to know what he was doing, though.

When everyone stopped, he ended up only two car lengths in front of her, she could see his face through her windshield reflected in his mirror. Skin the color of hickory. Deep brown, clearly regal. Cheek bones framed by an expertly tailored beard. Seemingly sensing her appraisal of him, he removed his baseball cap to show his head, bald, bare, and gleaming. Though invisible, the crown was clearly at home there. Before she got out of the car, she caught his eye and knew that he could see her too. He smiled, and the sun itself seemed to gleam off his teeth. He felt like a magnet.

Stay focused, sis! Her internal voice scolded her. As she was walking and looking for any clue that traffic would get moving soon, she could see his eyes lock on her watching her walk in his direction. Seeing no signs that they would be moving forward in the foreseeable future, she suddenly seemed to make a decision. With a smirk in his direction, she stopped short, stared in the mirror for a beat, and walked back to her car.

She rolled her tinted windows up and cranked up the air. *Might as well be comfortable.* She let her thoughts drift to her date night and decided that a little pregame fantasy wouldn't hurt. She may as well make good use of her time, right?

She moved her head from side to side, stretching her neck, while simultaneously unbuttoning her shirt from top to bottom. The screen in her car immediately registered a video-call request. Her left hand reached to massage her now naked breast, bra long disregarded during the commute even before traffic, while the right hand reached to hit the button to stop the noise. Glad both hands were now available to help her relax, she cupped both breasts in her hands and squeezed them rhythmically.

Her favorite playlist boomed its bass through her speakers, shadows starting to darken the highway and the car. *May as well take advantage of the scene.* As she squeezed her breasts in time to the rhythm of *Maxwell's Urban Hang Suite*, her hips started swaying from side to side, and a familiar slow heat started to grow from between her legs. Without even thinking about it, her forefinger and thumb slid down to her nipples and began alternately squeezing and rubbing them. This just intensified the heat and generated an additional source of fire.

"VVVVVRRRRRRRRRMMMMMM!" Good thing she had the car in park. Her foot hit the gas as she lifted her hips to pull up her skirt. The car gratefully didn't budge, but she could see the beautifully made truck driver look back in his mirror. All was well . . . and the skirt now rested at her waist.

She could feel the lace and satin combo of her raspberry-colored panties. They reminded her about date night. Maxwell continued to croon in her ear as she rubbed the softness of the fabric and her skin beneath. Her hips moved as though she were on the dance floor with her favorite boo grinding close. The warmth grew to a more urgent heat. The grind didn't stop. It intensified as she grinded her ass back, imagining her dance partner, and forward against her hand, further stoking the flames.

Her right hand was still busy massaging one breast and then the next seemingly crying out for attention. Her hand occasionally slid up her chest and neck and through her braids, as she could imagine her dance partner would . . . or her lover.

As the song changed to a more insistent and rapid beat, her hips moved in time. She didn't think she could keep it slow if she tried at this point. Her fingers desperately pulled the fabric to the side to dip her fingers into her wetness. She stared through the windshield as her body exploded, no longer in tuned to the music. This time, her moans made their own verse and chorus.

She licked both lips and exhaled a long breath as the spasms of ecstasy slowed and stopped. Careful of her feet, she lifted her hips again and slid her skirt back down her hips. With another, more satisfied roll of her neck, she buttoned her work shirt from bottom to top.

Perfectly timed, cars around her that had turned off their engines to wait began roaring to life with the expectation of joining the slow creep to a moving pace that had started in front of them. She looked in her mirror just to make sure she looked put together as her heart slowed to a resting pace. All she could do was smile back at herself, grateful that she had put her formerly wasted time to good use.

As she moved, now rapidly down the highway and then the road to her house, she found herself strangely disappointed as the eighteen-wheeler she had been stuck next to turned off on a different exit. She had enjoyed their short travel together; he was definitely easy on the eyes. She wondered where he was going, and was he thinking of her right now.

Shae pulled into her driveway, thankful her brutal commute was over. She smiled as she walked to the table and saw both a note and a vase of roses on the kitchen table. The note, from her teenage son said, *Have to work tonight, then staying over at Ed's house like we discussed. Love you!* She was so proud of his responsible communication. She had to take these wins where she could during these teenage years. The card on the roses, she knew what it would say before it was even in her hands. The roses and cards were routine but still appreciated. "Can't wait to get home to you! It's date night!" There was no signature because there was none needed.

He had been gone for a couple of weeks, but she knew he'd be home to her any minute. She jumped in the shower so that she would be ready to greet her road warrior as soon as he walked in the door, whether they decided on a date night out . . . or right there in the living room . . . and the bedroom . . . and the kitchen . . . . and possibly the enclosed back porch.

No sooner than she stepped out of the shower did she hear the back door slam. She wrapped the fluffy towel around herself and hurried to the kitchen to greet her king. Closing the distance, she could see her road warrior hurrying to her. Hickory skin seemingly gleaming, she could tell he had made a stop at the barber shop on the way home to get his head cleanly shaven and a fresh line. Not yet a crown atop his head, but the negro leagues baseball cap that she had given him for his collection last year held the spot.

"Couldn't wait to get home to you, sweetness. That was some show you treated me to."

"Just a little sneak preview. You knew what was going on. The video call was a cheat."

Shae heard the deep chuckle that she had missed during these long nights imagining him on the road without her and smiled. "I needed to see a close-up. We both almost wrecked the cars ahead of us with me trying to peek through that windshield."

"Well, I hope you didn't get your fill. That was just a little appetizer to hold you over until dinner. You know it's date night."

He took a step back and admired the dripping wet body before him. No doubt, he was ready to snatch her up and drag her to the bedroom caveman style, but he held his composure.

"Of course. I've been thinking about date night all day. I made a reservation for us at Le Roy's Steakhouse. Let me hop in the shower real quick, and we can be on our way."

As Shae bent gracefully into the passenger's seat of the Mustang, he allowed himself a longer look that slid over each of her generous curves. She knew that before long, his hands would be all over them, handling those curves even better than he wove that big truck in and out of traffic, but she was grateful for the restraint that he was showing so they could make it out in the city. She loved how he showed her off and was more than happy to oblige. Building up the anticipation was one of their favorite things about date nights. By the time they got home, the fire they both felt at seeing each other after being away for a week at a time would be stoked to an inferno. It might take all night to put it out. When it was all said and done, date nights were her favorite nights of the year.

THE BLOCK

He walked up and down the block, swinging a machete at his side casually like it was a briefcase. It scared me to walk by him, but crossing the street would be too obvious. I was scared because he was watching me too. I walked by, feeling terrified with my eyes low while increasing the pep in my step. I walked briskly while saying a very swift, "Hey, Mr. Goodwine.

"What's up, young blood?" That was the brief exchange and I could barely breathe because my nerves were so bad.

He was mythical to me in real time. He was larger than life, he was extremely scary but generous in a bizarre way. Mr. Goodwine was a true oxymoron.

I've watched him for years. Whispers about his corrupt dealings, his well-kept wife, and ruthlessness intrigued me. Hushed conversations about his acquired wealth and untouchable nature baffled me. No one dared question him to his face.

He owned everything on the block promoting entrepreneurship, giving back to the neighborhood, and recycling the dollar within our community. Mr. Goodwine was the only black man I knew who owned real estate and was a landlord who owned several local businesses: a bodega, a liquor store, a laundromat, and a car wash.

What frightened me was he also contributed to the destruction of humanity on the block. His entrepreneurship was a cover for his drug business that ravished the community. He was the only black man I knew with so much power. I watched his tenants get thrown out on the street for spending their rent money on drugs that his street soldiers sold them. The businesses cleaned his money. I grew up watching this tyrant. As a young adult, he fascinated me; I still feared him, still avoided contact, but paid attention from afar.

Mr. Goodwine and his crew knew every family in the neighborhood. They knew I was an only child in a single parent home, and my mother struggled. They offered me work running the laundromat on the weekends. It was easy money making sure the customers were provided with quarters for the machines and clothes weren't left sitting in machines, preventing other customers from using them. The drop-off service kept me busy, and the money earned helped me pay for my extras.

They targeted me because they considered me a good kid and trustworthy. I went to school every day, wasn't a teenage mother, dressed modestly, and never ran the streets. This was a rarity in my hood. The girls thought I was conceited because I wasn't a fellow

hood rat, spoke proper English, and graduated high school. The guys
hated me because I didn't give them the time of day, ignored their
catcalls, wasn't impressed with their sneaker game, and made it my
business not to cohabitate with them.

Considering myself a loner I wanted better and deserved
better. I was determined to make something of my life. Breaking
generational curses, I was a freshman at Columbia. I stayed home to
cut cost. I stayed to myself, which was why I caught his eye. I stood
out like a sore thumb in my neighborhood in a good way.

In the beginning I was nervous to work in the laundromat
because I didn't want any parts of trouble. My nervousness and
hesitation made him assure me I had nothing to worry about, so I
believed him. It scared me to tell him no. He was right. It was the
best job a student could ever have.

My workday was from noon to six. My shift was late enough
for me to sleep in on the weekend but ended early enough to enjoy
my day. I was a hard worker and devoted to my job at the
laundromat, showed up every weekend on time, kept the floors swept
and the machines clean. The money was always right at the end of
the night . . . until it wasn't.

I kept coming up short, while counting the money after
closing one Saturday night. How was that possible? I was careful with
the money. Scared shitless, I counted and re-counted. While
explaining to Mr. Goodwine that his money was short, I realized we
were alone. All the customers were gone for the night. The front
door was locked and the open sign was turned off. We were standing

in the backroom by the safe so no one would see me back here with him from the sidewalk. I started to panic.

Holding my breath, scared of the repercussions, I stood awkwardly in the lounge area where he held private meetings. I could not explain the shortage at the end of the night. It was basic math. A solid twenty exchanged for two rolls of quarters. How was I a hundred dollars off? Loyalty was everything in his world. I had no idea how this would end. I watched him beat a man to a pulp and open slap a woman across the face for much less. His intense glare made me nervous.

Inhaling his cologne, watching his chest heave up and down, I realized he was in good shape to be in his fifties. There was definition under his fitted, white wife beater. My chest was tight, also rising and falling with my shallow breathes. I had firm breast, perched, sitting up high. At the age of nineteen, with no kids and well known among the young kids as the neighborhood Double-Dutch champion, my body was firm.

Sweat trickled down my cleavage under my white v-neck. I noticed sweat beads slowly trickling down his face. It was warm. It made me wonder if the sweat was my internal temperature rising or the result of the environment. I then felt a bead trickle down my leg. Was I peeing on myself? Why did I wear a tennis skirt today? I was paralyzed, not sure what to do.

I whispered, "Mr. Goodwine, you can dock my pay for the hundred dollars."

He whispered, "It's not about the hundred dollars. I wipe my ass with hundred-dollar bills, young blood."

I knew that. He was wealthy . . . I think. I knew he was at least hood rich. I forced myself to swallow a dry lump that sat in the middle of my throat. Feeling even more nervous now, my palms felt sweaty, and my hands shook as I held them together, clasping them in prayer position. I then asked quietly if we could count the money again. He grabbed me by the throat and said, "We counted the money three times!"

Stumbling backward against the wall, I opened my eyes expecting rage and possibly a brutal beat down. A year and a half of being a good employee came down to this moment. I looked in his eyes and saw an intense gaze. Struggling to maintain eye contact, I decided to act quickly. I grabbed him by the sides of his face and kissed him aggressively. My lady parts were on fire. His tongue tasted like whiskey. My hands roamed under his shirt, gently massaging his massive back. He dropped the grip from my neck and landed his hands on my breast. I felt a gentle squeeze, then his thumbs gently gliding across my nipples. Mr. Goodwine didn't look as scary to me in this moment so I took my hands from under his shirt and gently forced him onto the hideous velvet plush couch that furnished his lounge.

Feeling powerful in that moment, he grabbed me by my sides and bit my chin, licked my neck, squeezed my firm ass, and moaned quietly in my ear. I ran my fingers through his short wavy hair, kissed his face, and took his shirt off. I took my shirt off swiftly while he unclasped my bra. In that moment, I wanted skin-to-skin contact. His body warm while his nature rose through his khaki shorts against my panties.

I unbuttoned his pants, forcing them down and moving with lightning-fast speed. Wasting no time taking off my panties, he simply tore the thin material, destroying a perfect pair of new underwear. I didn't give a fuck. I just wanted to fuck. Fuck him . . . I wanted to for years.

In one motion, he placed me on his prize. I slowly eased my way down. My slick interior walls helped me glide down his pole. I leaned toward him using one hand to hold the back of the couch. My breasts to his chest, sweating and panting, I sucked his earlobe. He was murmuring something I could not understand.

Riding faster, his arms were under mine, grabbing the top of my back; my shoulders forcing me to accelerate my speed and travel into a euphoric state. I leaned back a little, one hand on the back of the couch, one hand on his thigh riding the ride of my life. Before I knew it, Mr. Goodwine lifted me up by placing each of his hands under my butt cheeks. With one palm flat against the wall, the other gripped the back of his head while he inserted his tongue inside of my jewel box.

Alternating his licking from front to back while tugging on my lower lips, lightly sucking my pearl, he sent me into a dream-like state. When I thought I would explode, he stopped and slid me back down on his rod. I lost my mind and went demonic on his dick. The release made my eyes cross. I looked down, and he was hyperventilating. We didn't bask in the moment. I noticed his couch was stained, ruined.

I got dressed quickly. Looking me up and down with one arm on the back of the chair, Mr. Goodwine said nothing. He just steadied his breathing.

I didn't care. I had no expectations for him to do otherwise. I got what I wanted. I stood up to leave, while allowing the missing hundred-dollar bill to fall from my bra.

It was folded neatly. I stepped over it and walked out of the laundromat.

Refusing to look back, I walked toward my apartment up the block.

DELIA NICOLE

UP THE COAST- II

*F*resh out of high school, I was anxious to go to school as far away from home as I could get. I worked hard for years so that an academic scholarship would take me and my dreams of living like Denise on *A Different World* as far as we could go. When I was accepted to Howard with a full scholarship, it was a dream come true. I left my small Idaho hometown and went to DC to have a blast and get a degree.

The academics always came easy for me, and now it was time to let my hair down. And let it down, I did. Three weeks into my second semester, I found out I was pregnant. Xavier and I were not exclusive, but we were consistent. We decided even though it was a fairly new term, we were going to co-parent our son and do the best we could not to allow our change of circumstance to stifle any of the huge dreams we both held for our future.

I had no intention of giving up all I had worked so hard for, but I knew I would need support and refused to move back home. I transferred schools before I started showing. My aunt had recently moved to Miami, so I enrolled at University of Miami. Before the ink was dry on the paperwork, I was accepted, financed, and moved.

Xavier and I maintained a relationship, but it was primarily centered around parenting. At first, he would make the trip to Miami about once a month to see Zay and check on me. This was satisfactory to me, between him and his parents, we were well taken care of financially, and my aunt was a huge support. I was blessed to be able to both be an excellent mother to my son and still enjoy the college experience.

Finally, when Zay was two years old, I was on the verge of graduation, and Xavier was situated in DC after having already graduated. Xavier and I fell into a perfect routine that allowed him to fly in and get Zay, keep him for two weeks, and then bring him back. As far as I was concerned, it was the perfect arrangement.

Two weeks before graduation, I got a call from a former friend at Howard who shared information about a job opportunity back in DC that could lead to other positions. Xavier and I were doing a great job with our co-parenting, and despite a few minor bumps in the road, we operated amicably. I reached out to him to let him know Zay and I would be moving back into the area, and he insisted we stayed at his house. It would give him an opportunity to see Zay on a day-to-day basis and give us an opportunity to get established. I said yes without hesitation.

Our living arrangement was so simple and convenient. Eventually, Xavier and I exchanged touches, then kisses, then finally decided this was too easy not to take full advantage of the relationship that was all occurring whether we put a label on it or not but a name anyway.

Though he wanted to formalize it by getting married, I was hesitant and maintained I was happy with us doing what we were doing. I liked Xavier a lot. But to be honest, his personality was not the driving force of our relationship. Xavier was beautifully and wonderfully made. This man looked like God hand-created him. All angles and lines, no rounded shoulders or pudges anywhere but muscles popping out from everywhere. When we met in school, he had a low fade with waves so tight it made the girls seasick. He had a trimmed goatee, but now he switched to a bald head and full beard, following the trends and his maturity. Then, as if all this wasn't enough, God had draped all of this lusciousness in pure silk the color of a new copper penny. To top it all off, he always smelled good. His cologne must have been made from pure pheromones because when I smelled him, I was always ready to rip his clothes off.

To be perfectly honest, I had been thinking about ripping his clothes off all day. Fortunately, he was on his Tuesday through Thursday weekend. I knew he'd be back to working 20-hour shifts by Friday, so I had to get my fill while I could. As I opened the door, I scanned the living room looking for him. I could hear the shower in his room running. I restrained my legs from running as well, but a quick power walk put me right inside his master bathroom, opening the door of the waterfall shower. I peeled my dress off in one motion and stepped into the shower with him.

Not a word was exchanged as I dropped to my knees and engulfed his manhood into my mouth. I ran my tongue from the base to the head of his long thickness and swirled it around as I once again filled my mouth. He let go of a soft moan but did not speak. Water was raining down all around both of us, but my rhythm allowed for small breaths as he grabbed the back of my head, thrusting softly at first and then with more aggression. When I felt his thighs trembling, he reached down and grabbed my arm. With no hesitation at all, he had bent me over the sauna bench in the shower and was stroking me from behind. He grabbed my hips with each hand, pulling me to him and releasing me in a delicious and erotic dance. His rhythm became more erratic, so I concentrated and pushed back with additional firmness.

Seeing that I was about to cause him to lose control, he turned me around and pressed my back to the wall. His muscular arms lifted me above his head as he tasted and devoured me. It was a good thing Zay was still at practice, or he would have definitely heard my moans turned squeals, turned full-on screams of ecstasy.

This dude was fine fine, and our loving was excellent. So why was this not enough? To make a long story short, Xavier was boring. He was watching paint dry or watching grass grow boring. You would think a young man with so much intelligence and attractiveness would be charming as well. Unfortunately, he could barely hold a conversation. Xavier was an amazing doctor and dedicated to his craft, which meant lots of research and even more boring explanations of medical terms, medications, and journals. Since we couldn't spend all day every day in bed, our more clothed times were less than exciting, to say the least.

***

"There she is!" boomed a voice that always made me smile. Before I could even lift my head, I was scooped up and enveloped in a bear-sized hug. After one good spin, he squeezed my ass and kissed me on the top of the head.

We walked the length of the concourse as he told me about his weekend at the hospital and all of the cases he had seen. Being an emergency room doctor was a job he loved so much but kept him busy most weekends and often throughout the week. As he opened the car door for me, he turned and kissed me on the cheek and told me how much he missed me this weekend.

"I hope they can give you some weekends off pretty soon."

I turned my head and gazed off out the window. "The project is still pretty full of cases; it seems like one thing after another."

"You know you can pull back some on this, right? We are doing pretty well. Zay is well set up, the house is almost paid off, both your car and mine are paid off, and in good repair, both your savings and mine are healthy and growing..."

"Let's not go into this again, ok, Xavier? You know that I love my job and all the irritation that comes with it. I hate being away from you guys, but now that Zay is busy with practices, meets, and activities and you're at the hospital more often than not, there's no reason for me to sit at home all by myself playing Mary Homemaker...." The last thing I needed was him pressuring me to quit working or even making too many inquiries about the number of hours that I worked.

"Calm down, hun, calm down. I just missed you, that's all. I know how you feel about your job. I'm just glad you're back."

I kept the reasons I needed to work at the front of my brain because I knew my life was only working as long as I was employed in this position. I knew I had gotten off easy in ending this conversation so quickly. Neither Okoye nor Xavier knew our relationships, our entire happiness, hinged on me maintaining employment and flexibility.

THE VISIT

*T*his would be my family first time meeting the princess. My mom was a senior executive for a non-profit agency, and at fifty-two, she had no plans of slowing down or retiring. Working sixty-plus hours a week only allowed us to spend time together once a year at best during the holiday season.

This visit was Thanksgiving. My sister and aunt decided to fly in as well. When I picked them up from the airport, they gave me the briefest hug I'd ever experienced and rushed to the baby's stroller. At the house, while my family settled in and gushed over the baby, I went into the kitchen to prep my Thanksgiving meal. I planned to make a feast.

I was so happy to have family in my house. It felt good. The doorbell rang, and I yelled for my sister to answer it. I wasn't expecting additional company; I assumed it was one of my neighbors needing a forgotten ingredient. Then, I looked up to see my daughter's father embracing my mom and my aunt. My mom and aunt loved that dude, and my sister tolerated him. They were telling him how beautiful Treasure was, bombarding him with all the beautiful outfits they purchased for her.

Andre abruptly stopped them and said, "Can you show me when we get back Sunday night? I don't have a lot of time, and my family is waiting on me and Treasure."

My mom gasped, my aunt clutched invisible pearls, and my sister said, "Say what now?"

Andre looked at me and announced, "Bryce didn't tell you guys? Thanksgiving is my weekend." They all looked at me in horror.

Treasure cooed. I shot back, "Andre, your family is local. My family just flew in from New York. Your family gets to see her all the time. Why can't we switch?"

Andre sneered, "You didn't talk to me about switching."

I stuttered, "I assumed once I told you they were coming that you understood."

Andre snapped back, "Yes, I understood they were coming, but what did that have to do with me?"

I hissed through gritted teeth, livid. "Can I speak with you upstairs for a moment?"

The ass wipe agreed.

I glanced at my mom. She looked as if she would burst out in tears. My sister stared at Andre like she contemplated catching a case, and my aunt stated she needed to go have a cigarette. I was mortified.

I gently closed the door to the nursery, shooting daggers at Andre. "What the fuck are you doing?"

Andre looked at me and rebutted, "What the fuck do you think I'm doing? It's my visitation holiday, and I am taking my baby! You fought like hell for Christmas. Claimed that was your favorite holiday, so per your demands, you have Christmas. I settled for Thanksgiving."

"Fuck!" I yelled. "You're telling the absolute truth. I did beg the mediator for Christmas."

I softened my tone a bit. "Shit." I continued, "I did fight for Christmas. My sister could not take off for Christmas. The hospital needed her, so when my family changed their visit to Thanksgiving, I thought nothing of it. Any other time, you would comply with whatever I asked, so I assumed this time would be no different."

Andre frowned.

"Please don't be angry and difficult. I understand where you're coming from. We always had an amicable relationship regarding the baby. Why can't you be amicable right now? Your family is fifteen minutes away. They see her all the time."

Andre cut me off abruptly, yelling.

"Nope. The nice fucking Andre who you fucked over has left the mother fucking building. This Andre is playing by the rules. The rules that you set. Stop wasting my time. You're making me late for our family game night, which you know is our family tradition the eve of Thanksgiving."

"Andre!" This time, I was daring him, slightly turned on by his bad boy behavior. "You will not take Treasure tonight. The way you love my mom, you wouldn't do this to her."

Andre walked over to our daughter's walk-in closet, packed up two beautiful dresses, a couple of casual outfits, and onesies. He then grabbed a pack of pampers and wipes and proceeded to pack her blush-colored, monogramed baby suitcase.

I thought to myself, *this is an amazing show.*

"Excuse me," he said, while brushing by me, walking downstairs with me on his heels. He kissed my mom and my aunt. He didn't dare try to hug my sister, and he said, "Ma, Auntie Glow, I apologize for the miscommunication. I'll give you a few minutes with Treasure while I pack my SUV and get her car seat secured. I will try to have her back in time for you guys to see her again before you fly out Sunday."

My heat was rising. When he opened the door to go to his truck, my sister went bananas.

"What the hell is happening? I thought you guys were on good terms?" She ran and locked the door. "If he can't get back inside, then he can't get her!"

She was so hood. My sister was the type that would let him ring the bell and bang on the door all night and wouldn't give two shits about it.

I heard the garage door opening and stepped into the garage, which was adjacent to my mudroom. "Andre."

He acted as if he didn't hear me, and I walked up to him. "Andre," I said, grabbing his arm. He pulled away aggressively as if I was a pest.

I spoke. "Babe." Now, I was pleading with him.

Before I finished, he said, "Don't call me that."

"Andre, this is ridiculous."

He lashed out at me, causing me to take two steps back.,

"No! You're ridiculous. You are the reason for all this, so don't blame me. You screwed this relationship up. You got what you wanted. Deal with it," he said through gritted teeth.

"Andre, you are overreacting!"

"Really? Now, I am overreacting?" he yelled.

"Andre, please keep your voice down."

"Why? You're not my fucking girl, so why do I care about how you feel?"

I hollered our break-up was his decision. He told me our break-up was because of my bad decisions.

"If you hadn't told all our business to your girlfriends, we wouldn't be apart right now!" he yelled.

"You're overreacting," I said.

"Really? I heard you. I heard every single word you said. I heard you tell your friends how big my manhood was. I heard you tell them how I was soft and how I made love like a woman. I heard you tell them that you sometimes had to fantasize about other men because you were bored with me. How I have been using the same three positions in the three years that we have been

99

together and how I had to give you oral in order to give you an orgasm. Wasn't those your exact words? Let me make sure I quoted you accurately. 'Lord knows if he doesn't go down on me, I would never cum!' Wasn't that what you said, Bryce? Did I get that accurate?"

I was flaming. Andre was the best guy I ever had. He was kind, gentle, and a wonderful father and provider. I stated softly, "You listened to a private conversation during one of my girl's nights."

He said, "You called me."

I clarified, "I pocket dialed you, and you listened to me talking to my two best friends. I was not complaining. I was just being silly."

Andre said, "Bullshit! You were telling them how you really felt, and I am telling you that the hoe up the block from me—the one you claim dress slutty—is not complaining!"

I was shocked and heated. Shots fired! Papi would pay dearly for that with his fine ass.

"You crossed the line, Andre!"

"You obliterated the fucking line, Bryce."

"You can't take her, Andre!"

"Consider her gone, Bryce!"

I thought quick. "What if I gave her to you for Christmas?"

He retorted, "No. What if you gave me a blow job right now?"

I was flabbergasted. "I'm sorry. What?"

"Don't fuck with me, Bryce. You heard me. You can earn your family one night."

Shocked, my mouth fell slightly open.

"Your gonna have to open your mouth larger than that for him."

I was repulsed. "You're going to force me to give you oral sex?"

"Stop tripping. I ain't forcing you to do shit. You have a choice. Stop wasting my time. You can choose to blow me . . . slob, spit, and suck on it like your life depending on it. That will buy you one night. Ride and buck on it like a fucking savage, and that will buy you two nights. Make me shed a mother fucking tear, call for the man upstairs, and knock my ass out for the night, and you can have the baby for the entire holiday weekend."

I started tearing up. He was treating me like I was a whore. I was humiliated, and I wanted to strangle him until the doors of hell opened and took his soul. He brushed past me and went in the house. Two minutes later, he placed the baby in the car seat.

"Take her back in the house," I whispered.

Andre was now being sarcastic. "I'm sorry, what? You made a decision?"

"Give her back to my mom."

Acting like a jerk, he didn't even take me to his place. He parked on my wooded dead-end street and made me perform on the back side of his SUV like I was a prostitute instead of the mother of his firstborn child.

My damn knees were killing me, but resting them on the gravel was not an option. Dude was tugging back and forth at my ponytail, and when I tried to tell him that shit hurt, that my hair was real, he shouted and told me to shut up and take it. I could barely breathe, and he forced me to keep my eyes open and look up so I could watch his sinister ass enjoy my disgrace.

Then, this nut had me bottom-up, dangling out the back seat of his truck. He slapped my behind so hard my entire ass was sore. I felt at this very moment that he truly hated me. Angry sex did not properly describe the pounding my womanhood was taking right now. I imagined how funny it would be if a coyote ran out of the woods and bit him in the ass. He then flipped me over, and I ended up on top of his lap in the backseat of the truck. It was a rough ride, but I was determined to tough it out. This man was strong and had me feeling like I was having an out-of-body experience.

The next morning, I woke up feeling hungover. I turned to my left, and Andre smiled at me. He was happy, smiling, and while he kissed my lips, I could feel that I was glowing.

"What did you tell my folks when you brought Treasure back into the house?"

"I told them we talked it out, and I agreed to switch holidays. I then apologized to them for seeming unreasonable in the beginning."

Concerned, I asked, "Do you think it was cruel that we brought them into our role playing?"

"Nah," he said nonchalantly.

"What's cruel is the way they judged us for having a baby without being married, actively shaming us for living in separate homes. Since we are happy, we will continue to do what works for us. I'm not jumping through hoops to please anyone but you."

I straddled him, kissed him, and said, "you're right, baby. What's next? I'm thinking I'll be a correctional officer, and you can play an inmate on death row."

DELIA NICOLE

MEET MY GIRFRIEND

"*So*, what are you thinking about?"

"Nothing really…"

I give him a lingering sideways glance…

"Ok, just thinking about what we bout to do." I reply

"What about it? You having second thoughts?"

"Nah, nothing like that, you just really be making shit happen
for me

"You know, I do what I can do," hubby says with a smile.

He blows it off as a joke, but as I look back over, I think,
Damn, I love this man. I glanced back over and my eyes rest on his
thick lips, I think, *Damn, I love fucking this man.*

We pull up to the hotel, and as the valet takes the car, I think
to myself, I will no longer be a virgin when we head home. Ok, I'm
far past technical virgin status, but not in that way at least.

The road trip was not terribly long, but we were both ready to hop in the shower and get dressed for the evening. In a twist, we, actually he had planned and researched so that we could have drinks, smoke a little, and walk around the area. After a quick call to say we made it, we turn the shower on and got ready.

Dripping wet, he steps into the room to grab his clothes. I'm standing at the balcony, with my back to him, undressing for my shower. I can feel his eyes on me, so, I turn around and sneak a peek. Suddenly, he's not the only one dripping wet.

"Come here real quick," I beckon from where I stand with a little smile.

He looks at me and says, "What's up?" but begins walking towards me.

I don't answer, just watch him coming closer. That walk. Damn.

I don't speak as he finally reaches me, simply bend to my knees, and immediately put his thickening member into my mouth. He makes a sound that's somewhere between a moan and a chuckle. As I lick to the tip and then slowly down to the base, I looked up at him as he watched me take his manhood all the way down my throat, all traces of chuckle leave. His breathing becomes more irregular as I continue to swirl my tongue around the tip and then quickly devour him whole.

Abruptly, he reaches down and grabs my arm. Before I realize what is happening, he is snatching down my panties and stroking me from behind on the balcony. Well, between the breeze, the view, and the stroke game, I am coming in seconds.

Showing tremendous restraint, he smacks me on my ass and gives me a little push. "Go head and get in the shower, just a little appetizer for both of us."

Reluctantly, I move the direction of the shower and go ahead and begin getting dressed. *More to come*, I say to myself, attempting to show some restraint of my own.

Not long after I added the finishing touches, I hear both of our phones ping a notification. He looks at his phone and then at me. "Ready to go?"

I nod and walk towards the door.

Downstairs, introductions, and gigs are exchanged with my new friend. We finally decide where to go for dinner, and we're off. It was a little farther than planned, so we decide to take an Uber because...heels. The lady's feet are purely decorative, not meant for walking tonight.

Of course, while we in the Uber, he starts a conversation with the driver. It's what I love most, and get annoyed by, his ability to connect with people so easily. That leaves my new friend and me an opportunity for some whispered acquaintances.

"I was worried I might feel a little shy, but I feel so comfortable around you."

"Likewise."

"Where yo bra at, sis?" my friend asks me and softly pinches my nipple.

"Aw, I must have forgot it..." I reply as warmth radiates through my body. "How about yours?" I say as I rub my hand over and cup her breast.

"Yeah, me too," she says quietly enough only for my ears.

Dinner is filled with good food and fun conversation. As the drinks and meal are wrapping up, it is clear that we are all trying to figure out the next move. I'm not even sure when or who decided, but we summon the Uber to be taken back to the hotel.

He goes to her car to grab her bag, and we head up to the room.

As though we planned it, we immediately head to the balcony and light up a blunt each.

"Match?" she says and smiles. We giggle, and trade blunts. We smoke in companionable silence. Standing close enough to touch, but not before long, I hear the door slam.

"You tryna hit this?" she asks him. He raises an eyebrow at the irony but simply nods.

I notice that what I'm smoking has burnt out, so I walk back into the room to get another in rotation. As I'm walking back to the balcony, the door opens before I can reach for the handle.

"Aye, take those pants off before you come back out here."

The sound of his voice reawakened the fire that was lit earlier. I don't say a word, just slide out of my jeans and stroll out to the balcony in my thong and crop top.

As I walk to the rail, he grazes my ass, then grabs it roughly.

"See, didn't I tell you my wife has a fat ass? It's firm, too. Feel it."

She slides a cool hand around me and cups my ass. He smacks it and then slides his fingers inside me. I gasped, but it doesn't escape my notice that the wetness that has built up allows him to slide two fingers right in.

As though rehearsed, she unzips my top from the back and begins raining small, soft kisses all over my breasts. My grip on the railing tightens, as do my walls. I feel my body begin to tense in preparation to orgasm. The second her tongue touches and then sucks in my nipple, I begin to shiver and release. I watch with trembling knees as she walks closer to him and licks my juices from his fingers.

"I know I said no kissing, but damn, I didn't know your lips would be this juicy. Can I kiss you?"

I don't answer, just place my lips gently on hers. She kisses me hungrily, nibbling and pulling at my lips, just like I like. I move my mouth down, lower her shirt and begin to lick and suck her nipples.

"Go in the room," he says, simply but firmly.

Without a word, we all walk into the bedroom. When we arrive, I notice that we are all in various stages of undress.

"Take that shirt off," I say to him, noticing that's all he has left to remove.

"Nah, fuck that, come here." I make a pouting face but move towards him. It doesn't stay long, though. She is standing face to face with me, so I pull her shirt off over her head slowly.

"Teach me how to touch it, I say..."

She looks at me almost in surprise and then takes my hand. She dips my finger into her wetness and then swirls it around her pearl. I'm a quick study. I begin stroking and rubbing her pearl with two fingers and then slid them inside her and beckoned her to cum for me. As she gasps, he grabs me around my waist and pulls me to him, ass in the air. "Don't stop," he commands and begins fucking me from behind.

By this point, I can hardly tell who is moaning. My fingers continue navigating this completely foreign but also shockingly familiar territory, and my head drops face-first into the blanket. He backs up abruptly and judging by how ragged his breathing is, I can tell he almost came.

"Come, make her cum," I say softly but insistently. She scoots over and we lay on each side of her. He takes over my rubbing and stroking, and we both begin sucking and licking her nipples.

"Oh, yes. Just like that. Right there. Yes, I'm going to cum for yall!" she exclaims...then does.

As she catches her breath, we both reach for him and lay him down.

No words are exchanged as I position myself almost as an extension of him. I cup his balls with my hand and turn and look at her. "Let me watch," I whisper.

She bows as though in prayer and begins to lick and suck his dick. I watch, checking out her technique. I lightly squeeze his balls. Her head game is pretty good. Sexy. But not as good as me.

By this point, I am impatient for my turn. I'm happy to share though. We lick from the bottom to the tip on opposite sides. We take turns taking him into our mouths deeper and deeper. I can feel his body tighten and his movements becoming more irregular—his sexual communication signals as familiar as my own at this point. I slide him in a little deeper.

"Take his soul, sis," she giggles, like the world's best hype man.

I oblige, taking him all the way down my throat, feeling him growing harder and starting to throb. When I hear him gasp and see his toes curl, I sit back in satisfaction.

I turn back to her, kneeling in front of me, and begin to touch her again. He watches, catching his breath.

"Teach me how to lick it," I say to her. This time, she smiles and lays down in front of me. He watches silently, as though this was the premiere, he had been waiting for. I put my head between her thighs and thought about how I love to be licked and try to provide a mirror image of it.

"Lick slowly around the clit. Suck it gently and let it slide out of your mouth. Use a wide tongue to lick down the clit. Use a narrow tongue to slide just inside her walls. Go back up, circles around the clit." She didn't say a word. In true form, I thought out each move as I did it, imagining being on the receiving end, making me even wetter.

I hear her squeak, then her body convulsed. I smile proudly but don't stop, and now that I know what I'm doing, I am able to freestyle. Before long, I feel thick fingers slide inside me and feel myself grinding hard on them. My river starts to flow at almost the exact time as hers. She cums hard, and I keep going as she squirts all over my face. I am surprised and turned on by the sweetness of her. I don't know what I expected.

Without really knowing how or who did so, I look up to find that I am lying on my back. He begins fucking me roughly, but I am throwing each stroke back. She touches, runs, and licks me everywhere. I feel like I am floating on a sea of something heavenly. Ok, so this is what they are talking about, huh.

He suddenly slides back and sits down on the corner of the bed to watch. I'm not sure if words have been exchanged or not. I was in my own little orgasmic world. His manhood is exchanged for small, soft, firm lips, and it feels like seconds before I am cumming again. I feel her tongue and lips providing a perfect imitation of the motions that I was just making. They are equally as successful.

Finally, she slides up next to me, holding me and caressing my breasts. Softly, this time, and he rolls up behind me, holding us both. Our breathing slows and becomes one as we doze in a heap of exhausted bodies.

***

The sun hits my eyelids right before I feel a familiar pair of lips brush my cheek.

"I'm headed out. I have to go to the office."

I sit up and hug her.

"Thanks, I had a great time," I murmur.

"Me too. Talk to you soon!"

He grabs her bag and walks it back to her car. I sit up and thought about breakfast.

"Well, did you like that?"

"Yeah, I liked it, but..."

I look quizzically at him.

"I noticed that you didn't cum," I say to him

He shrugs. "It was different. We already have amazing sex, so..."

I agree and then pull the blanket back so he could join me in the bed. I slid his shorts off. Without discussion, I roll over onto him and rode him. He squeezed my ass and pushed harder into me. I feel him throbbing already, so I give it a little squeeze the way he likes. It backfires, and I feel myself cumming in waves. He never stops stroking, but I feel it becoming harder and erratic. One, two, three orgasms back to back. I throw my head back and moan my 'hotel sex' moan. One last stroke, and he is filling me with his cum, and we are both trembling. Damn. I am one lucky chick.

"What you want for breakfast?" I ask him as though he did not just fuck my brains out for breakfast.

We both smile and get ready to leave this adventure and on to the next.

REVERENCE

*W*alking down the corridor toward my husband's office made me excited. I had such great energy and was bursting at the seams with joy and wanted to share that with him. The fact that he brought nine more people into the family's business was astonishing. I was so proud of him; he worked hard on this new endeavor, and growth was necessary. Our team was proud of him, and I was ready to wrap my arms around him and smother him with kisses.

Bursting into his office startled him, but watching the woman standing a tad bit too close, invading his personal space, irritated me.

"Oh, hey honey, wha..what are you doing back here?" he stuttered.

"Am I not welcomed into any space that my husband holds?" I questioned while glaring at her.

"Absolutely, Baby Cakes, you're such a kidder, you know you are my rib, and wherever I am, you are welcomed to follow," he replied.

The female smoothed the front of her too short, too tight dress as she looked at her feet. My eye contact held steady, and I mentally read her from head to toe.

"Well, Ms. Davis, our session is up," my husband spoke as he showed her the door, almost closing it on her heels while he hugged me.

"Let me guess. She was crying on your shoulder about issues with her husband?" I fumed.

"Something like that, but honey, you know I can't divulge what is said in here, and you also should be comforted in the fact that you will never have to worry about your husband doing anything unethical."

Upset with myself for giving him an out, I changed the subject. Counseling was my husband's job. I imagined the things discussed caused emotional sessions.

I wanted to take him out for lunch, but he was booked and couldn't go. Disappointed, I left and went home to celebrate alone. One bottle of wine and one Xanax later resulted in me passed out across my couch in a drunken stupor. I did not know when my husband made it home.

***

Bringg, Bringg.

The phone went straight to voicemail. It was 7 the next

morning. *Where could my husband be?* I checked his location, and the results showed *'husband not found.' That's weird; maybe his phone is dead. Maybe he already left and headed to the office.* I dropped him a text and figured it was time for me to take a warm shower.

Sitting on the heated toilet seat, I allowed the hot water from the shower to steam up the bathroom. The door cracked open, and I looked up at my husband wearing the same clothes from yesterday.

"Where have you been all night?"

"What are you talking about, baby?"

"You have on the same clothes from yesterday, Devin. It's obvious that you did not come home!" I sneered.

"Really, baby? Is that where we are in our marriage? You have on the same dress from yesterday also."

"That's because I fell asleep last night in the den," I explained.

"I know, baby. I came in last night, and you were sleeping peacefully. I decided to go into our office and write my dialogue for next week. I was inspired, and since you were out like a light, I decided to pound it out."

"Oh, well, why didn't you answer your phone?" I whispered, a tad bit embarrassed.

"I cut it off last night and had it upstairs in the bedroom charging. You know, baby, every so often you need to cut off your phone so that it can upload your updates. Can I join you in the shower? I have to head into the office here shortly."

"Absolutely, baby," I said, relieved he hadn't taken my accusations to heart.

Later that day, I figured I should surprise my husband with his favorite treats. I felt horrible about jumping down his throat earlier, and it caused me to spend a hundred dollars on an edible arrangement.

Sweet smelling perfume filled the air, tickling my nose causing me to sneeze. My husband's secretary walked out of his office, looking down while wiping her mouth. My unanticipated presence made her jump, causing her breasts to jiggle in her low-cut dress.

"Achoo! Achoo!" Her perfume was not kind to my nose.

"Mrs. Barlow, are you okay? Can I get you some tissue?" the secretary yelled.

"I'm not deaf. I just have fragrance allergies!" I barked. *Good grief, why was she so loud? You could hear her a mile away.*

"Hey, Baby Cakes," my husband laughed, peeking out his office door, smiling.

"What are you giggling about?" I snapped. I didn't see anything funny.

"You, my dear, making a ruckus while trying to surprise me once again. Epic fail, but I am excited to dig into the treats you have for me in your hands."

Guiding me into his office and taking the fruit basket from me, I looked around. The smell of that stinking perfume made me sneeze three more times, irking me to my core.

"Why did you have your office door closed?" I asked.

"Reviewing my schedule and looking at payroll, one of my staff members had a discrepancy we needed to find and discussing someone's financials are private, baby."

"Gotcha," I mumbled. I wasn't sure when I became an insecure female, but I had to stop assuming things.

The week flew by, and I was excited about our church's revival. It was my favorite time of the year, and I needed the restoration of God's presence in my life.

Adorning one of my new custom-made dresses, I wanted to get my husband's approval on my attire before I went to the revival. I wanted to look elegant but not over the top. The dress was purple, my husband's favorite color, and somewhat simple. What made it stand out was the tailored fit and the body that filled it out. I knew this dress would please my husband; it was conservative but sexy.

Arriving at his office door, I walked in on loud moaning. His chair was turned backward away from the door, but from the shadow, I could see someone in between his legs, bobbing their head vigorously up and down. I gently closed the door, making my way down the hall, tightly covering both my mouth and nose, trying not to make a sound.

I ran into the bathroom and locked myself in a stall while

trying to calm my breathing; I could feel a panic attack rising inside me. My mind was racing. Feeling sick, with trembling hands, I held on to the top of the stall door. My head swirled, and I was dizzy; I sat on the toilet breathing in and out, slow and steady until my heart rate returned to normal.

While sitting on the toilet, I thought about all the times I felt like my husband was unfaithful. Devin Barlow had me thinking I was paranoid, overreacting, and suffering from low self-esteem. After all, he was successful, extremely handsome with beautiful chocolate skin, a swimmer's build, thick curly hair, and a cleft chin embedded into his chiseled face.

Considering myself lucky, I decided to suck up my tears and figure out how to handle him later. Surprisingly, no tears fell. Heaving slightly with a heavy heart, I knew I couldn't go home. I committed to my church family to attend revival this year. Normally, I would watch revival and church services via live stream. Reluctantly, I went into revival, greeting a bunch of friendly familiar faces, blocking out what I witnessed earlier. Sitting on the front pew, my heart seemed to be pounding out of my chest, I was disturbed. Trying to gather my composure, I knew I was about to give the best performance of my life.

After reading off a long list of unnecessary accolades, they announced the pastor, and he entered the pulpit with a thunderous applause. My husband walked toward the podium with his arm in the air like he was the pope. Infuriated, I shot daggers at him, secretly praying he fell off the stage and snapped his neck.

"Thank you all for joining us tonight for our 3rd annual revival here at Wayside Springs United Church of Christ. I also want to acknowledge the first lady of Wayside and the love of my life, Kaiya Barlow; you guys know this is a sweet treat because she's normally watching from behind the scenes."

Sitting as stiff as a stuffed duck, I reluctantly waved. At this very moment, I was ashamed to be his wife. Devin knew I hated a lot of attention, and large crowds made me nervous. My anxiety started to creep in. Feeling the urgent need to pop a Xanax, I thought it would be inappropriate to take one.

"Stand up, sweetheart, and greet our congregation," he bellowed.

I stood up and smiled as I stepped out to turn around and wave to the congregation.

"Achoo! Achoo," I sneezed. Bumping into me was his damn secretary. She was always in the wrong place at the wrong time. I felt a pat on my thigh and looked down at a beautiful, curly haired, brown-skinned boy.

"God bless you, First Lady," his squeaky voice chimed.

"Come on, baby, let's find grandma and get seated," my husband's secretary walked off hastily with the child in tow.

Holding my chest, my heart felt like it was going to jump out and land on the pew beside me. I am sure the applause and the cheers had the congregation thinking I was overjoyed with emotion. I smiled and sat back down. I wiped my eyes and focused on regulating my breathing. Tears flooded my face. A deacon handed me some tissue, and I thanked him. I closed my eyes and said a quiet prayer.

The prayer was asking God to keep me from killing a bitch. The tears were because that baby boy with that dimple in his chin was the spitting image of my husband.

AT MY ALTAR

It was so ironic, all my life I had been the good girl. From the patent leather shoes and the lacy socks to the velvet dresses, I had spent my childhood in the pews of various churches. Sermons washing over me full of repentance and damnation, I had no intention of following the path to hell that was laid out so clearly. Why would I engage in these activities so clearly outlined before me if the exchange was life in eternal flame? It seemed silly even to consider these unrighteous deeds.

Now, look at me. I lay sprawled on the bed, an ancient scripture ready to be read, explored, consumed. I watch as he prepares for this imminent worship. I know the preacher I had gazed upon for so many years of my childhood would not approve. I knew he would tell me these actions damned me to the fires of hell. So many years had passed, so many experiences had occurred, so I no longer believed this was a direct road to hell. As a matter of fact, it may take me closer to heaven.

You lay the carefully folded towel at my feet.

In its unfurled state, it is a magic carpet, primed and ready to take me anywhere I want to go

Now, it forms the basis for the altar you have begun to set.

You place both knees on the altar as you kneel before me

Could this be a prayer, as you grab my thighs and push me back into a reclining position on the bed, the vulnerability in position is clear on both ends.

You bow your head, but the words come out of my mouth, not yours.

Not a list of requests or a litany of gratefulness, though make no mistake, I am more than   grateful. A gasp and then a moan escape my lips and are chased with a stammered and elongated ffffffffuuuuuuuucccccccccckkkk.

Pretty strong language for a prayer.

As your head moves in time to my now quickened breathing, it is clear that the offering you have brought much satisfies your goddess. Her pleasure is demonstrated in the gathering of the seas between her thighs.

Hips, thighs, ass, move in rhythm to the worship songs you sing. Your hands grabbing, squeezing, holding, allowing no drop of these seven seas to escape your attention or consumption.

You raise your head to look upon my face. The remnants of the wetness you have inspired drips down your beard like blessings raining upon the earth. I am pleased. My body undulates in yet another response to the worship you heap upon me.

You lower your head once again as our now combined forms sing songs that I personally deliver to heaven. It can't be my imagination. Choirs of angels seem to have joined the singing; the melodies reverberate all throughout my body.

When I can no longer hold the bounty of praise you offer, my body seems to reach high for a deity higher even than myself and then fall back to the bed in exhaustion and satiation. Your still dripping beard and a hint of ivory teeth from your smile of self-satisfaction culminate this blessed experience.

My legs continue to tremble as you arise from your altar. You lean down and kiss my lips to leave a trace of the wetness you have so expertly coaxed out of me. You leave me to wash your face as I regulate my breathing. It seems as though I hear church bells in the distance, ringing the sweetest Amen...

DELIA NICOLE

THE BOND

*B*ouncing up and down like a professional equestrian, I was proud of my straight back and my awesome formation. My legs bent at a ninety-degree angle, and I planted my feet firmly and securely on both sides, letting the weight of my body measure evenly on my horse. I enjoyed the ride while my hair bounced up and down in the wind, sweat glistening down my face while my orgasm crept up inside of me.

"Aww, man, baby, I am coming!" Screaming and squirming like he had transformed me into something supernatural caused me to snap out of my trance and open my eyes. Looking down, I watched my sister's newly appointed boo thang making the ugliest screw face ever! I closed my eyes, then felt a drip of liquid run down my boob.

Did this fool spit on me? Yuck, is that his sweat? What the fuck is this wet shit running down my boobs? Eww! Why is he spitting, yelling, and sweating like a heathen when I was the one doing all the work?

Ready to conclude this ride, I tried to dismount him, but his massive, calloused hands firmly gripped my sides, keeping me in position. My beautifully measured north and south hip strides turned into ferocious uneven roll-bounce twerks. I think dude became possessed, and at this point, I wasn't controlling my own movements. I flopped around like a rag doll, like an infant before they get their full head and neck control.

Damn, why am I tasting blood? Did he just make me bite my freaking tongue?

Making matters worse, this fool threw me off him the way a bull violently tosses a matador. I almost hit my head on the ceiling fan before landing on the corner of the bed, then on the floor.

Thump.

"Ouch!" I yelled!

"Oh shit, my bad, babe. You alright? I couldn't hold onto you any longer. I exploded and lost control. You okay?"

Yeah, fool.

"Yeah, I'm okay. I just have a little pain from where my pinky toe hit the corner of the nightstand, but I think I am okay."

Damn, I hope this fool didn't break my toe!

Aiden lost all points for losing control.

How the hell did he throw me like that? I am 165 pounds. Shoot, I am now light-headed. Did I hit my head on the ceiling fan blade?

Unable to decipher what was happening because the pain in my little toe was taking over my entire body, I was disoriented for a minute.

"R-r-r-ronc, shshshsh, r-r-r-ronc."

Seriously, is that him snoring? Is this man asleep? You have got to be kidding me. Does he have narcolepsy? He was just talking.

"Ugh!"

Irritated, I just stared at him. In the dimly lit room, he looked like he was a 6'2" alien from outer space with a dead eight-inch tentacle lying flat, extending from his lower midsection while sticking to his left thigh.

Getting up from the floor, I checked my foot. I limped to the shower and prayed when I got out, his spaceship came and deported him back to whatever planet dudes like him came from. No such luck! After a twenty-minute shower, the alien was still lying there. Little did he know, in about another thirty minutes he would have to get up and get out!

I sat at my huge mahogany desk in my office tired as heck trying to jot down some notes. I knew I would have to pay for my sexcapade last night. Three hours of my damn life I could not get back. Thank goodness I had no meetings on my calendar. I was literally in a daze with my head bobbing front to back every so often as I stared at my computer screen.

Thud!

Damn.

While nodding off, I hit my head on the silver, long-armed desk lamp that extended outward, which hung low over my computer's monitors. This caused me to burn my forehead from the hot metal lamp top.

"Ouch!" I yelled. *Damn.*

That was it. I was going home. I would tell my employees I was working from home for the rest of the day. Hopefully, that burn wouldn't leave a mark. Driving home, I thought about what my sister preached about the quest to find love. Chase had all these methods she believed helped you find your true love. Amazing sex was mandatory for her. Not sure what she was looking for, but I just had her man, and Aiden wasn't it.

Pondering the last conversation, me and my sister shared, I thought, *Would I ever have true love? Would I ever have a passionate lover who made my heart flutter, or is that all just a myth?*

Thinking back, I had several loves but not that great true love. Not the love that takes your breath away and knocks your socks off.

Reflecting on a good lover named Charleston I had in graduate school, I was curious to know what he was doing now. Instead of taking my breath away, he suffered from stinking ass breath! To this day, I never found out what caused his halitosis; he had beautiful teeth, and none of them were rotten. I made sure he went to the dentist to get them checked out. Unsure if it was his diet or his bowels were backed up and the odor permeated through his mouth but damn! I just couldn't take it. Trying to keep his breath fresh I almost went broke keeping him stocked with breath mints.

This man had the audacity to tell me one day that maybe it was my breath I smelled and not his! My eyes bulged and almost popped out of my head, then to make the matter worse, he always tried to kiss me with his poop-smelling breath. His breath smelled like he sucked on shitty diapers all day long.

After a couple of months, and a couple of rounds of me jumping up and down on his pogo stick, I had to let him go. I just couldn't take it. All the good looks in the world couldn't trump proper hygiene. I would have at least given him a little leeway had he admitted there was a problem and he was interested in getting it fixed; however, his ass was in denial. I left his denying ass right where I found him. I felt sorry for his mouth. Those beautiful white teeth deserved better than that.

Then, I thought about Malachi. Malachi was one of the nicest guys I ever encountered. He was just a big, emotional nerd. Malachi had no street cred about himself. He cried during sex, which turned me off; he cried during our arguments, which made me feel weird; and he cried during love stories, which bothered me deeply.

Don't get me wrong. I don't mind a sensitive man. For instance, if you cried in church because the message resonated with you. That's understandable, but when you tell me *The Notebook* is your favorite movie of all time, it makes me look at you sideways. My sister and I considered that a chick flick.

I had to let him go. He cried about that shit too, but after seeing how often and how easily he cried, I still kicked his ass to the curb with a box of Kleenex. I couldn't take it; however, he's extremely attractive, wealthy, and a nice guy, so I am sure he is laying in between the next set of legs, crying on her breast. There are plenty of women who will have him. I am just not one of them. I don't have time for that shit!

Finally, there was Hudson. I thought Hudson was the one. I wanted Hudson to be the one. Chase and I agreed he was almost perfect. His skin was perfect, his teeth were perfect, his body was amazingly perfect, and he had just enough swag to turn me on but not enough to make me feel like he was a thug. The perfect mixture of street smart and book smart—not one attribute overwhelmed the other. They mixed and mingled perfectly.

Looking back at that relationship, the only problem I couldn't overlook was he was an exotic dancer. He worked hard and made a ton of money, but I couldn't get past all the attention and all the women he came across.

Not sure how to introduce him to family and friends, I always tensed up at the thought of someone asking him what he did for a living. I tried with Hudson because he had potential; Hudson had hopes and dreams and a vision for his future. He was very smart and financially savvy; he owned his house and several rental properties. Hudson also wanted to own a business flipping houses and selling real estate. He was using his good looks and capitalizing off his great body because he knew he could not dance forever, and one day, he would have to leave the stripping career behind.

I offered him to be my afterhours man, but he would not accept that. It's funny men have booty calls and side pieces all the time, but when the tables were turned, guys couldn't handle it. This was the very moment I realized dudes caught feelings too.

At this point in my life, I was honest and open about my needs, and since Hudson couldn't accept my offer, then Hudson was out. I had way too many dudes trying to holler and did not have time to debate how I wanted to fill my bed. Chase said I lost a good one; I often wondered if maybe she was right.

Tonight, I prepared myself for Cain, multitasking as I boiled some cinnamon sticks on the stove downstairs while rubbing a lotion oil mixture all over my body upstairs. I wanted everything smelling nice when he arrived. The house was dimly lit with candles while slow jams played in the background.

Ding dong. My neck snapped upward.

Yikes, he's early!

Ding dong.

Ding dong.

"Damn! I'm coming!" I yelled.

Impatient bastard.

Opening the door, dude rushed me immediately.

"Fuck, ma, you look good. Damn, you smell good, ma. What's good? Take that off. Take that robe off now."

Cain took his clothes off frantically.

What the hell is the hurry?

"You wanna eat?" I asked.

"Nah, Imma eat you, ma!"

"Yo, these candles is nice. They add atmosphere and shit, ma. You taking too fucking long. Come here!"

Before I knew what happened, Cain bent me over on the dining room table with his head deep in my ass.

"Argh! Slow down, babe. What's the—"

"Shut up!" he cut me off abruptly.

His rugged ass beard scratched the inside of my thighs. Thank goodness I had rubbed them with oil, if not, I would probably be bleeding right now. Cain ate me out so roughly I found myself crawling across the table trying to get away.

This motherfucker caught my ankle, dragged me back, and started pounding my insides sideways. My damn neck hurt while the side of my face was flat on the cold, hard wooden table. Trying to brace myself with my hands to prevent him from snapping my fucking neck, he went into third gear, banging like a jack hammer at a construction site causing my head to throb.

This is what I get for sleeping with another one of my sister's boyfriends! Shit, I have got to stop this shit!

Reaching my hand back, he slapped it hard.

Ouch!

Why is this fool acting like he just got released from a ten-year bid?

Cain placing me on my stomach gave me relief because my neck ached.

"ARGHHHH! What the hell?"

"Shut up, ma! It's just a little hot wax."

Pounding away, this dude convinced me he had a battery pack up his ass. Twenty minutes later, he was done.

"I gotta go, ma. Good looking out. I'll holler at you later."

Walking beltless down the hall, exposing his boxer briefs, Cain slammed my front door and was gone. I wasn't sure what I just experienced, but it was definitely unforgettable.

That next afternoon, I met my sister for lunch. I was nervous to see her. Chase walked into the restaurant confident, beautiful, and poised. Her voluminous hair bounced up and down, her jeans looked like they were painted on, and her caramel skin was radiant against her mango top.

"Hey, sissy." She embraced me tightly. Returning her bear hug, I smiled, inhaling her lavender-scented perfume. I loved her so much and was grateful to have her as a sister.

"Chase, let's order because I need to talk to you about some things, and I am going to have to tell you some hard truths."

"Chance, it can't be that bad." She smiled. Rubbing my arm, she said, "Sis, lighten up. It will be okay. Give it to me straight. You know you can tell me anything."

Taking a deep breath, I thought, *Here it goes.*

"Oh, my God! You ladies are absolutely stunning," the waitress squealed, startling us.

"Thank you," Chase and I said in unison.

"Wow." The waitress laughed. "You guys are identical I can't even tell you apart." She stared at us awkwardly.

"We hear that all the time," we both said at the same time again.

The waitress was beside herself with giggles. Chase and I were accustomed to people making a big deal about us being identical twins.

After the waitress gathered herself and took our orders, my sister grabbed my hand and squeezed it.

"Alright, Chance, give it to me straight. I want your honest thoughts. After fucking both Cain and Todd for me, which one should I keep and try to pursue a relationship with?"

UP THE COAST- III

I lay in my bed, and just like every morning, I have to wonder what day it is and who I will find next to me. These two conditions were dependent upon each other. When I felt the beard rubbing against my shoulder and the strong, thick fingers holding my thigh, I knew that it was somewhere between Monday and Thursday.

As I started orienting myself for the day, I realized that it had to be at least Tuesday since I ended up staying over in Miami an extra night on Sunday. It was in fact Thursday, I realized. I went down my mental list of things to do today as Xavier stirred beside me. A few visits, plenty of paperwork, and a flight tonight at ten. Nothing unusual.

This was a rare day that he had the chance to languish in bed before racing off to the hospital. We seemed to enjoy our nights together more than our days, and I could take full responsibility for that. Despite the three proposals that he had given over these some fifteen years, I gracefully declined each time, telling him that I loved things being the way they were. Simple, focused on our son, fun. I knew he was not the man who I would want for my husband, but our arrangement was working out well for us . . . well, me.

As I went to sit up and get my day going, he grabbed my wrist. "Lay back down with me for a few minutes. That computer will wait." I moaned my indecision. There were plenty of tasks on my to-do list, but the time we spent was well worth it. He snaked an arm around my waist to assist in my decision making. It worked.

As I slid back down into the bed next to this delicious man, I pushed all thoughts of relationship progression, stimulating conversation, or the lack thereof, and hurtful secrets to the back of my mind. With the way he was touching and rubbing my body with such familiarity, he made it so easy.

His arms were steel bands as he pulled me close to him. All traces of sleepiness now gone; he used his strength to move my body according to his demands. My re-entry into bed signaled my consent, and if there was any unclarity, my responses to his touch confirmed. X grabbed my ass and pulled it close to his body; I could feel that he woke up with me on his mind. No gentle kisses, he propped himself up on his elbow and sucked, then nibbled on my neck and shoulder until I worried that he would leave passion marks on them. He then flipped me over on my back, nudged my legs open, and slid right into me. The sound I made was somewhere between a gasp and a moan.

It was like I could feel him up to my stomach. He thrust slowly at first as I got accustomed to his presence, then began stroking faster and deeper. My hips caught his rhythm and began meeting him with every thrust. One of his strong arms slid up and squeezed my breast roughly and pinched my nipple between two fingers. Leaning on his other hand, never stopping or slowing his thrust, he moved his hand up farther and squeezed my neck on both sides. I didn't make a sound, only arched more so he could see the effect he was having on me. Xavier leaned down to my face and kissed me roughly, then made a grunting sound that let me know how much he was enjoying dominating me in this way.

Feeling like the kryptonite to his superman, I was re-energized by his sex sounds and slid to the side to flip him over but was surprised when I was the only one who flipped. Nonplussed, I placed both hands atop the headboard and pushed my ass back on him as he stroked me long and deep. He pulled me up vertically with him for a moment to change the angle and slid one hand up to my neck as he slid the other down the length of my body, roughly fondling my breasts, squeezing me to him, touching every part of my body as though confirming his ownership. I placed my hands back on the headboard as he grabbed a handful of my curls and pulled just firmly enough as his other hand guided my hip first away from and then back to him. I exploded once, twice, three times as he stroked me into the land of paradise. Finally, after my fourth explosion, he followed me, and we fell onto the bed fully satisfied.

"Who needs coffee?" I said to him as I regulated my breathing, kissed him on his forehead, and got up and jumped into the shower to start my day.

After that delicious start, my day seemed to go by like a breeze. I handled impatient clients, demanding bosses, and even uncooperative technology like a total boss. Before I knew it, the sun was starting to go down, and I was getting ready to head to the airport.

This familiar flight was smooth and relaxing. I fell asleep and dreamed of the memory of this morning's session. By the time I woke up, my panties were wet, and I was surreptitiously looking at my seat neighbors to see if I had been moaning in my sleep. I felt a little guilty, but I knew this would only serve as an accelerant to the loving that was coming.

***

Before I could knock on the door, it slid right open. Okoye was standing in front of me in her satin robe and nothing else.

"I hope you looked through the peephole. I could have been anybody," I said to her with a smile as I walked in to take her into my arms. She tipped her head up slightly to invite me to her lips; my RSVP was immediate.

"I felt your energy before you made it in the room," she replied between kisses. Okoye was always prepared for my arrival, but I could see that she had taken extra care today. There was a beautiful and delicious charcuterie board on the coffee table, and *Love Jones* was playing on the TV, which we had seen so many times that she had soft music playing over as background music.

I dropped my bag by the door, washed the road dirt off my hands, and proceeded to wrap them around her. She led me to the sofa and began to unbutton my shirt and peel it from my shoulders.

"How was your day? Mine was great," I murmured with a chuckle.

"I need you now. We'll talk later," she replied as she uncharacteristically and aggressively pushed me down onto the couch and began to peel my leggings off. I kicked off my Crocs and raised my hips to help her endeavors. Okoye's mouth moved from my mouth and covered every inch of my face, then neck. I left the moment only for a second to wonder if Xavier had indeed left any evidence of his presence, but when she continued and moved on over my shoulders and then breasts, I exhaled with pleasure and relief. Her mouth covered my peaks and suckled softly, then she used her teeth to truly announce her arrival. Meanwhile, her hands rubbed all my curves, and made each and every piece and part feel appreciated, necessary even. I reciprocated in kind as her robe fluttered uselessly to the floor.

When my body felt like it was fully aflame, she slid first one, then two fingers down to rub my pearl. My body felt as though it was levitating. She rubbed in slow circles, then increasingly in pressure and intensity. Right as I was on the precipice of release, she slid these same, pleasure-giving fingers into my wetness. It increased exponentially as I reflexively attempted to sit up, and my body began undulating. It was as though she beckoned my orgasm with her "come hither" motion in my womanhood, and it responded without hesitation.

I grabbed her thigh and pulled it toward me, flipping us over. It was my turn to make sure she knew how good she was making me feel. I hovered over her body, kissing her from head to toe. She was writhing in anticipation while enjoying the teasing, and she could barely wait for me to push her to the brink. I slid down her stomach, leaving a trail of kisses and stopped right at fat ma. I knew her body so well that even after only a year of dating, her smell, landing strip, and wetness were etched in my mind. I placed feather light kisses on her inner thighs, on her mons, still teasing and tempting. Finally, she grabbed my hair, lifted her hips, and started grinding right on my face to show me how much she wanted me.

This was the second time today that my hair had been the key to an orgasm, and I provided and received as I turned my tongue into a rhythmic tornado. Her moans and squeals mounted as I continued swirling my tongue around her pearl, then into her slit. Round and round, in and out, up and down. Lips, face, tongue, fingers, and even used the little bullet vibrator that I saw she had strategically placed on the coffee table. By the time she slowed her movements, my breathing was shallow, and my face was soaking wet, just how I liked it.

I didn't have time or interest in guilt as I remembered I enjoyed both of my lovers immensely today. She sat up slowly and smiled a lazy and satisfied smile. "So, how was your day?"

Deceit

THE RIDE

*P*rofiling in the back seat of my buddy's new Audi Q7 SUV, I felt the car stop abruptly tilting me forward.

Honk, Honk, Honk.

"Get your nasty ass out of the middle of the street. The light is green, you bum!"

I looked up in horror, checking to see who my classmate was talking to. Obviously, she didn't get the memo. Two school-aged white girls talking shit out of a new car would not only get your ass whopped in Brooklyn but your car jacked also!

Two older women were crossing the street. They were making gestures in response to all the yelling and screaming coming from the front seat of our car.

"Who's that, guys?" I asked from the back seat. "Do you

know them?"

"Eweee, heck no! Look at them ghetto bitches. We don't know people like that. We don't know anyone in Brooklyn but you. Luckily, you're cool enough for us to drop you off at home, otherwise we do not drive our asses into this borough." Honk! Honk! "Walk faster, you sloppy bitches! You caused us to miss the fucking light!"

My classmates were behaving in a way that exclaimed we were heathens.

The two women were old enough to be our mothers. One of them looked old enough to be our grandmother.

I watched the women closely. One of them must have had quadruple-D breasts. They were massive, and she was not wearing a bra. Her breasts hung low, her nipples protruding downward, the top-heavy woman had on a t-shirt dress. It was dirty, short, and thin. The white dress was stained while a lit cigarette hung from her lips.

She walked toward the Jeep, cursing and slurring her speech. The woman was drunk. Her stench made us cringe.

The driver, who was my cheerleading captain, said, "Back your stink ass up before I pepper spray you!"

The woman had no teeth. She mumbled something vulgar, stumbled closer to the Jeep, then burped. My classmate threw her drink at the woman yelling, "You bum bitch!"

I flinched.

"Guys, let's just turn right and go," I stated. "I think these women suffer from mental illness or something. Honestly, you don't have to go through the light. I know another way to get home by turning down Bedford Avenue. It may even be quicker."

My classmates giggled. The passenger spewed. "Their drunk asses aren't mentally ill. They are ghetto-ass, welfare-ass, drunken-ass bums."

There was something about the way she said welfare ass and ghetto ass that made me cringe. It was the condescending tone and the entitlement that reeked through her white privileged skin that irritated me. The way she felt about my borough and the disregard for an elder who was a woman of color upset me.

In that instant, I regretted accepting this ride home. I was exhausted, and riding two trains and a bus was much less appealing than driving from Queens into Brooklyn in a comfortable air-conditioned luxury vehicle.

My feet were on fire. All the stomping and cheering during our three-hour practice made my feet throb, not to mention the full day of school before cheerleading practice started.

The downfall of going to a school so far away was the commute. One hour and thirty-five minutes each way got old quick. However, with the way my spoiled classmates were behaving, I felt like the bus and train would have been a better option.

Queens was like a different world from Brooklyn. Bayside, Queens, was a wonderful escape and gave me another perspective of my city. There were beautiful brick single-family homes with garages. Most blocks flaunted manicured front lawns and backyards and a lot of trees. What attracted me to my high school was the massive campus across from a lake. I was grateful to be accepted. It was the first time I experienced a location outside of my neighborhood of Bushwick.

In Brooklyn, I lived in an apartment building where a mishmash of weirdness resided I observed every day. I hated it and dreamt often the key that opened the door to my home opened only my door, not a front door shared by twenty-nine families because the building had twenty-nine apartments.

There were single parents, couples with no kids, single men, single women, old people, young people, and unfortunately a lot of undesirables. The undesirables brought the entire building down. The front door was always broken, allowing vagrants to hang in the halls. The intercom was merely for appearance. Most of the time, it half-worked, which didn't matter since the door stayed open.

Thugs hung out on the steps and looked at you sideways when you said excuse me and tried to walk by, they wouldn't get up; they would just move their legs over. If I was wearing a skirt or dress, it became very uncomfortable to have to walk up a narrow flight of steps with hoodlums sitting there looking at you like you were prey.

Sometimes they would use the halls as a bathroom with golden liquid puddles in the corners. It was horrible. Not to mention the graffiti that decorated the walls. I was so ashamed to call this place home. In my heart, I knew my mom did the best she could but damn. Why the hell couldn't she have a better job that offered us better housing?

This damn light took forever. I listened to my classmates say some of the nastiest things about these two women.

"Hey! Hey! Why is your hair half-braided and half-matted? Is that the new style in bumhood?" They giggled as if they were comedians, like Lucy and fucking Ethel.

"Why are you walking on the back of your sneakers? Your crusty heels couldn't fit in them? What is that crusty white shit on the back of y'all's feet?"

More hysterical laughter. I saw nothing funny. Internally, I was enraged.

I was happy for the tinted back windows because I was ashamed right now. Both of my classmates came from upper middle class two-parent households. I never dreamed of having a car in high school. Honestly speaking, I prayed that my mother could make the rent every month.

Finally, the light changed, and I was able to breathe. They dropped me off and I thanked them for the ride. Opening the front gate, walking up the steps, I looked back and waved. They drove off and as I watched them drive off, the door swung open, and a man said, "Who are you? What do you want? I hope you are not about to try and sell me some shit."

"No, sir. I was wondering if Christine was home," I said.

"Nobody named Christine lives here!" he barked.

Apologizing, I descended the stairs to the stranger's beautiful brownstone and swiftly walked the three blocks to my home.

Humiliated from the entire experience, I searched for my keys to enter my building. It was a waste of energy because once again, the front door was broken. Running up the stairs, taking them two at a time, I burst through the doors, scaring my mom, causing her to jump. I collapsed in her arms crying.

"What's wrong, baby? Did someone hurt you? Were you robbed again walking home from the subway?"

I whispered a soft no. "I saw grandma on my way home. She was drunk again."

I disclosed everything that transpired with the exception of being dropped off at the wrong address because I was ashamed of where we lived. It was important to me that I didn't hurt my mom's feelings. I already understood the pain she felt being raised by an alcoholic mother.

"Did she see you?" my mom asked me.

"Not this time," I said. "She came extremely close to my window, but that's when Amber threw the drink on her."

My mom apologized to me for my experience, but her doing that made me feel worse for some reason. She wasn't responsible for my grandmother's bad choices. My mother was an innocent casualty in a cycle of abuse that extended generations before her.

Unfortunately, my classmates were casualties of inadequate

parenting. I now felt like an asshole. Why did I lie? Why didn't I stand up and tell them that was my grandmother, and she was sick? Why didn't I allow them to see my apartment and tell them that was what my single mother could afford and praise her for not allowing us to be homeless?

I loved my mom; I would not be apologetic about who she was. She worked her butt off, and she made sure we had food, clothing, and shelter. Fuck my spoiled-ass friends. They could kiss my entire ass. I would come clean and handle their asses when I saw them in school tomorrow.

Once again, I lied.

The next day I went to school. When they recounted the incident from the drive home, I jumped in and added my two cents about the two women.

Peer pressure was a fucking beast. I reasoned that at least I understood right from wrong. They told me how nice my brownstone was and went as far as saying they did not know houses that nice existed in Brooklyn.

While outrage brewed on the inside, I outwardly smiled and said, "Thank you. My dad is a chemical engineer."

WAITING GAMES

I swiped the wet rag across the table angrily with one hand while I balanced a stack of plates with the other hand. My love-hate relationship with this job was tipping dangerously low on the hate side today. Why was I bussing my own tables? Didn't we pay a heathy tip-share not to have to do this for ourselves?

"Move that big old thang out of the way!" Sherry said as she slapped my ass on her way past. I was definitely not in the mood for her bullshit today. Sherry had been my manager at Feasty's now for six years. I used to love working here, but when she took over, the only word I could use accurately to describe the way she impacted the restaurant's culture was toxic. Have you ever known a woman who got a position of power, then instead of using it to uplift and grow the sisters coming up behind her, she used it to dominate and abuse? If not, let me introduce you to Sherry.

"Hands off, please," I turn and say to her dryly. I would have loved to contact HR about her behavior, which was consistently inappropriate and abusive, but retribution was her middle name. They wouldn't believe me anyway. She was sweet as pie when corporate came around, and no one had the courage to speak out because they knew they'd have to deal with her when the suits were gone.

My words fell on deaf ears. She was already halfway across the serving floor.

I saw a host seating one of my regulars in my section, and it brightened my mood. This particular diner, Mr. Thompson, had been coming in for years, always alone, and was such a pleasure to serve. He liked to come in when it wasn't too busy because I always made time to chat with him a little. He was an extremely handsome older man. I would guess early sixties, but you know that good black don't crack, so he could have been anywhere from sixty to eighty. He rocked a bald head and salt-and-pepper beard that made even the young waitresses at the restaurant salivate.

Every Thursday afternoon, he came in and ordered the steak medium well with a side of garlic mashed potatoes and steamed broccoli. He ate only half of the meal every time, but he didn't take anything home except his dessert, a bread pudding with extra drizzle. Every Thursday afternoon, he asked for me.

"Be right with you, Mr. Thompson! How was your day today?"

He waved in greeting and sat down at his table.

After dropping my dishes and trash at the bussing station, I walked up to his table. Thursday afternoons were pretty slow, which was probably why he chose this time. Sherry was in the back, so I sat down at his table with him like I tried to every week for a few minutes.

"How has your day been, Mel?"

"You know how it goes, Mr. Thompson, same old nonsense. But I have been following your advice, so I can see a light at the end of the tunnel. I know trouble don't last always."

"Have you been following it all?" He chuckled deeply. Mr. Thompson shared wise advice about God, life, love, and money every time I saw him. One of his favorite quotes was "I'm retired, so I know everything and have time to tell you all about it."

"I'm trying to!" I smiled and responded. "You going to have your regular order today, Mr. T?"

"Is the sun bright and the sky blue?"

I made a big show of looking out the window to check, then as I saw Sherry coming from the back and looking around, I got up to go put his order in to the cooks.

Mr. Thompson was my favorite customer who helped me get through my shift with a little less angst. He always tipped generously by giving me a ten dollar bill and a gold coin—rarely the same one twice. Usually, he always reminded me to hold onto it for a rainy day, but today as he was finishing his meal, he stopped me.

"Melody, I almost forgot to tell you. I'm taking a few of my coins in to sell this week. You know I've been saving them, but the prices are up higher than I had anticipated, so I'm going to go ahead and liquidate a bit so I don't miss it. Have you still been saving yours?"

"Of course, Mr. T! I wouldn't dare do anything else." I chuckled as I recalled how many times he had reminded me to put something away for a rainy day.

"Ok, now's the time. Gold prices haven't been this high in years. If you still have two or three of them, go ahead and take them to the Gold Bureau and do something nice for yourself. You might even have enough to take a little vacation from here . . . just make sure you're back by Thursday!" He laughed and grabbed his bread pudding container.

Mr. Thompson had told me about advising young people for years about money management and investments and expressed more times than I could count his frustration that young people didn't seem to want to learn that kind of information or have the discipline to wait and be financially strategic. I laughed inside as I thought about how well I had been listening for the past five years. I thanked him and grabbed the towel and dish bucket. There was no need in me waiting for one of the bussers to come clean up the table, and I could see several parties at the host stand waiting to be seated.

Back at the cook line, some of the other waitresses were chatting when I walked up. "What were you and sugar daddy talking about today?" said Lex, another waitress.

"Now, you know I'm not even looking at him like that!"

"Whatever! I am! He is fine, smart, and his social security is paying out!" We all fell out laughing, mostly because I knew she was serious.

"No, actually, I was going to tell you that he said now is the time to sell some of your gold since the value is so high."

"We don't all have a big stash from our sugar daddies like you, Mel. But we'll get together what we can. I know he never steers you wrong, and you never steer us wrong."

It was so important to me to share the knowledge that Mr. Thompson always dropped on me with the other girls. I knew that everybody had dreams and aspirations beyond this place, and I didn't want to be anything like Sherry. I wanted us all to win.

The rest of the shift passed without additional incident. We laughed together despite the bitchiness of Sherry, the demanding customers, and all the additional work that was required from us.

The next morning, I woke up smiling, knowing that I didn't have to go into the restaurant until much later. I hadn't had a Friday off in forever, but today the restaurant was rented out for a party, and I was not one of the servers who had drawn the short straw for that shift.

I got up and gathered my coin collection. Mr. Thompson had said that if I could sell two to three coins that I would be able to take a vacation. I wondered how much gold was selling for that two to three could get me a vacay. I wondered what my actual collection would be able to produce.

Walking into the coin dealer that Mr. Thompson recommended, I pulled my rolling suitcase behind me. After examining my coins, the appraiser handed me a slip of paper and told me to take it to the cashier. My eyes bugged out of my head when I saw the number written on the slip. I had dutifully saved every single coin that Mr. T had given me on his weekly visits. Even though there were occasional weeks he missed, consistency was definitely his strong suit, along with money management, of course. That was about fifty coins per year, and over the course of my five years there, I now had 250 coins.

Since he told me to go ahead and sell some of them but not all, I had brought 150 with me. The cashier asked me if I wanted my funds in cash or a cashier's check. There was no way I was going to carry around $300,000 in cash, so I asked for the cashier's check. I just stared at it for the longest time. I've never had this much money at one time.

Before I could lose my nerve, I sent out a text to the girls: *It's time. Meet me at the new spot.* I made a few more calls to get everything situated. "Thank you, Mr. Thompson, and thank you JESUS!" I said aloud as I confirmed my meetings. By this time tomorrow, my life would be so much different. I was never afraid of a little hard work, but this time, I could already see the payoff.

Finally, I pulled up at my job at Feasty's. The girls were tidying up after the party and getting ready for a crowded Friday night dinner service. I could hear Sherry's voice already. It was like nails on the chalkboard.

Typically, I would just walk in and get my apron on and get to work. Today, however, I came in with a greeting loud enough for everyone. "Hey, y'all! Hey!" Sherry looked up and rolled her eyes.

"Girl, get on to the back and get ready to serve. Roll some silverware while you are at it."

"I'm not going to be serving tonight."

"Excuse me? Well, I hope you don't think I'm putting you at the bar."

"I'm not going to be working here at all tonight or any other night. Last night was my last day."

Sherry laughed. "Girl, bye. I know you need this money. You better hurry up before I dock your pay."

"I didn't want to do it like this, but you have been terrible to me, terrible to us. It's time for me to go. Don't worry—this won't be the last you see of me, though."

The look on Sherry's face was one of disbelief. "Whatever. More money for you sluts," she said as she gestured to the other servers.

"Actually," said Lex. "We are gone too." Lex walked up to me and put her cashier's check for $25,000 in my hand. One by one, the four other servers followed suit. Even though they didn't have a regular who tipped them gold coins, she had shared the info that Mr. Thompson had shared with her and made a nice profit off their investments as well.

"We're all out of here. You won't have us to steal from and abuse anymore," said Jennifer.

"Well get out then! All you ungrateful bitches can get out of here! I don't need you!" Sherry sputtered as one by one, her entire wait staff, then host staff, and bussers walked past and dropped their aprons on the host stand and walked out the door.

I couldn't have been prouder. As I looked to either side, I saw a lineup of six strong, beautiful, and now financially independent black women. Women who were now co-owners of our new restaurant at the former site of Feasty's. For the past five years, we had been meeting over drinks after work to discuss and use the information that my favorite customer had been so generously sharing with me.

Sherry's face when we walked into the restaurant in our suits instead of our uniforms would have been a viral meme. We walked into the private dining area and called a staff meeting immediately. We assured the wait staff, bus staff, cooks, and bar staff that they would be welcome to continue working at our place as long as they adapted to the changes in culture and procedures.

"The management staff, however, will be undergoing some immediate changes. Sherry, please meet us in the office at the conclusion of this meeting. Assistant managers, please wait here for your turn to provide statements."

Our plans were finally coming to fruition. All our hard work and patience was paying off.

We had already decided that our Thursday special would be the Thompson- A steak with sides of garlic mashed potatoes, steamed broccoli, and of course, a bread pudding to go. I couldn't wait to tell our favorite, honored guest exactly how it went down.

ELEGANCE

*W*alking confidently into the classroom alongside two mean
girls made me determined to show my young classmates a thing or
two about elegance, style, and grace. I had overheard the two teeny
boppers in the bathroom last week talking about the older people in
their undergraduate class. They said something about how pitiful
we were and how we should have finished school a long, long time
ago.

"Do you see the outfits they wear to class? You can tell
they are old, and what about how long it takes for them to answer
questions? Why do everything have to be explained 3 and 4 times
to them?" they snickered.

They said several other horrible things about us as I was
eavesdropping in the large stall on the end row while doing my
business. Peeking through the crack of the bathroom door, I
already knew it was those two sorority girls making the hateful

comments.

At thirty-two, I was considered one of the older people. There were four additional "mature" students in the class doing the same things as the traditional students, learning and trying to get our degree. I decided in the bathroom stall that day that I would stop going to campus in my workout gear and baseball cap and start dressing like a grown ass woman, the same way I did when I went into the office. Maybe that would change their perspective and garner some respect from them. They were fooled by my frumpy comfortable clothes I threw on for class.

My wardrobe was fabulous, so today I decided to change up my look and I put on a double-layered mid-length skirt that was camel-colored with a mesh tulle that had black roses embroidered all over it. I wore a fitted black cashmere top that had a bowknot at the neck along with my black ankle Louboutin booties. Tossing my traditional backpack to the side, I placed my laptop in my Louis Vuitton Neverfull GM bag and put my two-carat diamond studs in my ear. My long, thick hair was freshly washed and flat-ironed straight down with a part down the middle, and I threw my Dior glasses on to finish off my look. I was casket sharp. My classmates would wish they never called me old. So damned disrespectful. These young girls got on my nerves.

I was ten steps in when my four-inch stiletto heel got hooked into the hem of my skirt, walking down the stairs of the small stadium classroom. Instinctually, I hopped on one leg down two steps, trying to catch my balance and get my heel out of my hem when the ankle I was hopping on twisted, causing me to fall with my long arms flailing like a monkey who missed his branch jumping from limb to limb on a tree.

My Starbucks coffee propelled into the crouch of a student, scalding his man parts. He screamed, "AHHH! Bitch!" The hot liquid made him appear like he peed his pants.

The LV bag catapulted into the air like it was shot out of a cannon with my MacBook flipping somersaults several times before landing on the back of the head of a bald man who was considered one of the "older" people in class. That was the one thing that I disliked about my bag: it had no zipper to close and hold my contents securely inside. The older gentleman screamed in pain, holding his head with a knot blooming immediately. His scalp quickly started to reflect deep red bruising.

Several tampons tumbled out and rolled down the steps about three miles per hour faster than I rolled. All my snacks fell out, and candy went all over the classroom floor. My bottled water slid out, busted open, and spilled water everywhere. As I toppled down the rest of the steps, my skirt wrapped around my waist, exposing my granny panties I was wearing, which were comfortable for me during my cycle. Unfortunately, I had a wedgie exposing my bottom because my left butt cheek scraped against a nail or something rough on the steps as I toppled down.

My hair covered my entire face, and strands stuck to my lip gloss, temporarily blinding me. I heard what appeared to be my cellphone pouncing down each step, hitting the bottom level of the classroom floor, shattering into pieces.

I was beyond embarrassed as I lay twisted up like a pretzel, looking like an exhibit at the bottom of the classroom floor, the kind police outlined to demonstrate where the body lay. My professor, who was young and quite handsome, got up immediately from his desk, running over to help me up. While he ran to help me, I heard camera clicks and giggling, and someone yelled, "I'm recording this!"

My professor then slid on the puddle of my bottle water, falling on his ass, then accelerated, causing his wingtip shoe to stab me right in the side of my face. He then rushed to get up and stepped on my hair. I felt someone squeeze my ass while my head ached from Professor Watkins' massive foot going upside my head.

"OMG!" a couple of students yelled. Several came to offer their assistance, while my fellow older female classmate placed her jacket over my exposed bottom.

Eventually, a few classmates helped me up and placed me in a chair. Everyone asked me questions at the same time, which did not allow me to gather my thoughts. Out of the corner of my eye, I saw the two teeny boppers laughing hysterically and recording the entire thing on their phones. I knew they would. That's what this generation does. They capture everything to post on social media instead of offering their help and services. It was a great show for those two, and I was pretty sure I would go viral if I hadn't already.

Before I knew it, campus police and medics came rushing into the room. They wanted to place me on a stretcher and asked me what had happened. *Who in the heck called them?* Gee whiz, this was more of a spectacle than I could have ever imagined. I glimpsed over at the Bobbsey twins again giggling, snickering, and taking selfies. It was all so funny to them.

It looked like a disaster zone in the classroom. My elder male classmate was getting his head looked at. The male student was being checked for third-degree burns. My professor was getting his ankle iced, and I was getting a combination platter of services.

The police came over and told me they wanted to fill out an incident report. It was campus procedure. They asked me what had happened. By that time, I was crying. Several classmates, both young and old, told me it was okay. I would be alright. Sobbing and then hyperventilating, I was doing the ugly cry. The cops told me to relax . . . take my time. They didn't want me to be more upset than I already was.

Someone handed me some water. I drank it slowly, then through my tear-stained, make-up streaked face, I pointed toward the teeny boppers who were still recording and yelled, "One of them pushed me!" Everyone gasped and turned toward them. They were so busy giggling and probably watching their footage of my fall that it took a moment for them to realize all eyes were on them.

The police went over and asked them which one of them pushed me. In unison, they said, "Huh? We didn't push her."

Explaining what happened in detail I told the police how I had experienced their bullying. I told them how I overheard them age-shaming me, comparing me to a fossil, and how I shouldn't be allowed to learn with them. The police listened intently as I told them how they said I was slow and in their way. The police asked them if that was true. They both turned beet red and stammered and stuttered, "Some of that is halfway true, but not all of it."

The police looked at them and said, "So, you halfway pushed her down the steps?"

In unison, they said, "No, no, that part is not true. The part about us calling them old and slow was true."

Going into further detail I told them I walked into class with them, and I was walking cautiously because of my heels. I had a business meeting right after class for work, and out of nowhere was when I felt a nudge, and one of them said, "Move please."

One of the sorority girls' eyes bulged. The other started crying. I told the police they had been bullying me from the start of the semester.

Another classmate said sheepishly, "I have heard them say that Mr. Charles talks too slow and too long when answering the professor's questions."

A couple of other students then mentioned they did see them recording my fall. The police told them this was a serious offense and asked for their phones. Of course, the footage was on there. They went live with my humiliating experience. Then, one girl said, "I don't remember pushing her. If I did that, it was an accident."

The police said, "Was it an accident that you uploaded the fall onto social media as well?"

They asked if I wanted to press charges. I looked the girls in the eyes and said, "Yes."

The girls were mortified. Now, the tables had turned, and all eyes were on them.

I bet they will never age-shame again. Bullying was something I hated, I was bullied when I was younger because of my clothes and my lack of affluence. This experience led me to mentor girls who experienced bullying, and it was always the spoiled privilege girls who were mean. I would make an example out of the two in my class. They had no idea who they were fucking with because I could make a lie sound like the gospel.

I was a tad bit concerned for Mr. Charles, who took a laptop to the dome. He was honestly a casualty. My professor was fine, but he was a tad bit strict and graded harshly. I enjoyed watching his ass slip and fall.

Frat boy got lucky since I was aiming for his fucking face, but I missed, so his crotch got the hot coffee. I hated his pretty ass. He was so rude and drove his convertible sports car like a bat out of hell on campus. Once he nearly hit me. When I approached him in class about it, he told me I should learn to walk faster. Yeah, his ass got lucky I missed his face.

The iPhone was old; my real phone was protected in my

car. I would never carry an iPhone without the protection of an OtterBox, however, I made sure the water bottle was extremely loose so it could splatter and spill. The loose candies were for dramatic effect—I did not eat candy. I worked out five days a week, and I did yoga all the time. Thankfully, I would be fine. Bending myself up in a pretzel was nothing different from doing some of my yoga poses.

The granny panties were on purpose. They were like bikini briefs. Typically, I am a thong girl, but I refuse to purposely allow the young boys to see my firm ass for free. I did skin my knee and my elbow a bit. That will heal over time. However, the shoe to my face was a L I would have to accept.

Now, I am sure thing one and thing two will think twice before talking shit about anyone else.

Checkmate, bitches!

BACK TO MY ROOTS

*H*er smile hid a multitude of pain, as each parishioner walked past, shook her hand, hugged her, and told her how blessed she was. She wanted to scream and break out into a sprint in the opposite direction. Standing by his side, she felt shame, fear, and disgust.

Each church lady filed by commented on her attire and her make-up, never noticing the flawlessly applied foundation covered a black eye and bruises across her cheek. One bruise, a full handprint. She snuck a glance from the corner of her eye at him. As usual, he was smiling, self-deprecating humor, admittedly handsome, but with a temper that would make your head swim. She would know because his temper made her head swim more times than she could count when she found herself looking at him from the floor.

Lois tried to enjoy their time at church; it was the only time she knew he would be kind and loving to her. She knew she never had to worry about him cursing her out, calling her stupid, or worse yet, hitting her when they were in front of others. He would never tarnish his reputation in that way. The irony was rich.

As the sanctuary emptied, he grabbed her hand, but she knew to keep the pace. As they got to the car, he opened her door and kissed her hand as she sat down. She wondered if they would have a good day after all. They took the short drive home, and she had dinner on the table in less than an hour, just the way he liked it. As she washed her hands and face to sit down at the dinner table, he looked up at her and rolled his eyes.

"Don't nobody want to see that shit. You trying to make me feel guilty or something? You shoulda kept that make-up on cause your face could use a little help anyway."

Lois didn't respond. She kept her head down and ate her food.

"We are having a guest minister at church next Sunday. You know I'm not much for women up in the pulpit, but her congregation sent a sizeable donation. Make sure that you take good care of her and get her settled in at the hotel on Friday."

"Ok, yes, I will." What else could she say? Yet another person to pretend with. Another person to act as though her husband was a human reincarnation of God instead of the devil that she knew him to be.

***

When she pulled up to the Ritz Carlton, she was eager to take care of business and get back to the house. The good reverend was going to be busy at the church for several hours, so she was guaranteed some peace and quiet.

She recognized Dr. Lucretia Edwards from the photos in the flyer. She had an air of authority about her that seemed to tell people immediately she was important. As she emerged from the vehicle, a driver opened the door for her as several hotel staff grabbed her bags. Her voice was as big as her presence.

"Lois! Thank you so much for coming to meet me and make sure I got settled! I've been so looking forward to meeting you!"

Lois murmured her agreement and shook hands. "Pleased to meet you, Dr. Edwards."

"Doctor, nothing! Call me Lu! I hope we become great friends!" Dr. Edwards walked toward the building and up the elevator. She and Lois made small talk as they approached the elevator. Men with the bags and keys fluttered ahead of them.

As soon as they walked into the room, Dr. Edwards...Lu placed a tip in the hands of every individual that helped carry items and asked them to leave so she could get settled. Lois turned to make her exit as well, as Lu placed a hand on her shoulder.

"It's seemed like forever since I've had an opportunity just to relax and have some girl talk. I don't suppose you have some time to indulge me..."

Lois thought about those few precious hours available away from the good reverend but couldn't find it within her to deny this beautiful, smart, interesting woman just a fraction of her time. She loved the joyful energy that seemed to emanate from her and sat down in a nearby chair.

Lu immediately stood up and came and sat right beside her. She grabbed both of her hands and looked at me like she was a little girl, all traces of the commanding presence that she utilized with her staff not gone but put away on the shelf no longer needed. Blazer off, heels off, she looked more vulnerable and inviting.

Lois opened her mouth to speak, and a torrent of tears flew out. Lu let go of her hands and wrapped her arms around her shoulders. Lois sobbed in this virtual stranger's arms for no less than 20 minutes before she began to taper off with soft hiccups. She was embarrassed at the liberty she had taken with Lu, but her strong, slender arms around her and murmurings of support were far too comforting for her to pull away too quickly.

It was no coincidence that she had nobody. No one to confide in. No one to run to. No one to escape to. The good reverend had long since discredited her to friends and family alike. They believed in his innocence and goodness as though they were gospel, just as he had planned.

Feeling seen, feeling loved, and cared for was a luxury she felt she was starving for, almost without even realizing how much. She accepted Lu's embrace and made no explanations for her breakdown.

"This can be a lonely life. I was the first lady long before I was a minister in my own right. Thank you for trusting me with your tears."

Lois nodded numbly, cleaned her face, and the two began talking as though they had known each other for years. They traded hair horror stories, laughed about the types of personalities found at most any black church, and even engaged the hotel staff and other guests in a game of blackjack in the lobby. No gambling, of course. Neither of them brought up the crying spell from earlier, Lu's personality just seemed to draw people to her. She was fun, friendly, and her sharp truth-telling tongue was kind but to the point.

Lois didn't want to leave Lu's side, basking in the freeness of a new friendship that had blossomed unexpectedly. The hotel was beautiful, the company was welcoming, and the wafting smell of fried chicken and brussel sprouts with a side of macaroni and cheese made her feel as though she was right at home.

The smell of fried chicken made her suddenly remember...

"Oh shit!" she exclaimed, then looked at Lu in embarrassment. "I've got to go; I have to get dinner on the table before Rev gets home."

"Girl, he is a grown man! He can figure out something for dinner. Didn't he ask you to help me out this weekend?"

"Yes, but... I gotta go..." Lois knew that there would be hell to pay if she didn't have dinner on the table when the reverend got home from the church office.

"Until tomorrow then!"

***

Lois grabbed a box of chicken and assorted sides on the way home. She quickly assembled it to look appetizing. The reverend seemed to have something on his mind tonight; he was not as talkative as usual. Aside from a rude comment about the carry-out chicken being better than her cooking, he ate quietly and kept the conversation within his own head.

"Don't get too comfortable running around with that broad. I don't like her coming over here and thinking she is all that. I'll be glad when she's out of here on Sunday; she needs to stay in a woman's place."

***

The reverend had just closed the door to head to the golf course when the phone rang. Lu's voice was frantic on the other end.

"Lois! Do you have a hairdresser in town? This is an emergency!"

"Lu? Hi, I was just getting ready to head over. No, I don't have a hairdresser. I do my own hair."

"My hairdresser usually travels with me, and she was supposed to land an hour ago, but I just got a text that she went into labor early. I'm thrilled for her, but I was relaxing in the hot tub last night, and my hair looks like it's trying to escape my head! I don't know what I'm going to do. I can't show up to the brunch like this!"

"Calm down, no worries. I am pretty good with a flat iron, wig, or whatever you need. I'll help you out as soon as I get there."

"Are you sure this head is a whole situation?!?"

"Definitely. I got you."

***

Lois didn't even take the time to get herself looking first lady fine before she left the house. She grabbed her suit and hat, make-up bag, and hair tools and jumped in the car.

Before she and the reverend had gotten married, she was one of the hottest hairdressers in her small town. Her shop stayed filled with satisfied customers. The reverend had courted her lovingly, but when they got married, he demanded she close her shop and leave the beauty business. He called it a den of gossip and promiscuity. It was ironic he required she maintain her chaste but elegant look but would not allow her to use her talents to help others achieve the same look when needed. The only looks she had cut, curled, weaved, or waved in years had been her own.

When she arrived at Lu's hotel room, she was ready to get right to work. Lu stared at her and pulled her into a hug. Lu's panic stopped as soon as she saw her face. "Who did this to you?"

Lois couldn't believe she neglected to make-up her face to cover the evidence of the reverend's last temper tantrum. Her eye was still a little purple and green around the edges. The handprint on her face, fading and fuzzy at the fingers but still well defined at the palm.

She tried to laugh it off. "Girl, I'm so clumsy."

"No. That's a handprint. I know what that is. I've had those before."

Lois led Lu to the desk chair, where she plugged up all of her tools without a word. She hadn't lied about her hair being a hot mess.

As Lois added conditioner, detangled, brushed, and worked heat protectant through Lu's hair, she explained her story.

By the time he started actually hitting her, it seemed as though she was too involved to leave him. Without her even realizing it, he had stripped her of her family, friends, business, and her self-esteem.

Lois' hands seemed to move with a life of their own as she arranged Lu's hair beautifully and efficiently to look even better than when Lois had first set eyes on her. Lu was beyond grateful.

Lois told her entire story dry-eyed and devoid of emotion as her hands moved through Lu's strands. Her lips spilled these secrets that had been tormenting her for years. She never told this to anyone before, but after all the tears of the previous day, it seemed to spill out like a waterfall. She didn't know what it was, but Lu was so easy to talk to.

Lu preened in the mirror in her modest dress and new and very attractive coiffure, but Lois knew she was listening and thinking.

"I just wish I could find the courage to leave him. If the congregation knew who he really is, how abusive physically and emotionally, it would ruin him. I don't have any money, don't have any friends or family, and don't know how I would make it without him."

Lu hugged her again and gently held her hand for a moment. As Lois finished getting herself ready for the brunch, Lu sat there thoughtful, occasionally looking back into the mirror, and touching her soft, bouncy curls, frowning slightly over her new friend's situation.

***

The next morning, Lu arranged to send her driver to collect Lois at her home before service. Lu was going to leave for the airport directly after service, and since she would miss checkout time at the hotel, she had all of her bags packed into the car already.

She thanked Lu's driver as he helped gather her things and slid gracefully into the car with Lu.

***

"I want to thank the good reverend for welcoming me to First A.M.E. of Zion and to all those that were able to join us tonight. May you be blessed by the word and this service. I would be remiss if I did not share my most sincere gratitude not only to him but to the First A.M.E family in total for their selfless agreement to allow First Lady Clark an extended sabbatical. She will be traveling with me with my production team as the lead stylist throughout the remainder of my tour and possibly longer. I know she will be sorely missed, but I am glad she is allowing the Lord to guide her footsteps."

The good reverend started to rise from his seat and walk to the mic. He had a fake smile plastered on, but his eyes were blazing.

Dr. Edwards grabbed his hand and held it up in hers as though they had rehearsed this. Dr. Edwards started praying. While the rest of the church bowed their heads, She looked straight into his eyes and he into hers. "Lord, we ask that you take complete control over these hands. We ask that you guide every movement and every intention behind them. We pray that you touch Reverend Clark's mind and heart so that he knows that every single thing that he touches is of you and covered by you. Our God will NOT be mocked."

He had the decency to drop his eyes in shame. "Yes, she knows," her eyes communicated to him.

She wished she could be a fly on the wall when he walked into the house and saw that all of her things were gone. All of her church attire and the few small personal possessions she owned were placed neatly and carefully into Lu's car and were probably aboard the plane already.

The timing of Lu's visit couldn't have been more perfect. Her former hairdresser had already notified her she would be taking time off once her baby was born, so now Lois was going to be her temporary live-in stylist. With the handsome paycheck, this would land her, the opportunities afterward could be endless. "I may even open another shop," Lois thought to herself.

She finally had hope. She could finally dream again. His hold on her was finally over, her prayers finally answered.

PLACING MY MAN ON PAUSE

I did not want his ass, but he refused to leave. This on again off again relationship was for the birds. He was a liar and had me feeling things that upset me. Dealing with him coming in and out of my life for the last four years left me exhausted, and I wanted out. I wanted to be done.

One moment, we were hot and heavy, and the next moment, he put me on chill with an overlay of frost. He irritated me so bad until it never fazed me when he would decide to ghost me. It became a problem when he kept coming back, and I had no choice but to let him in.

Some people would describe what was happening to me as abuse, especially since he felt the need to make me bleed several times each month. At times, he caused me to have headaches so bad that all I could do was lie down. This relationship was toxic as fuck! I would just cry thinking about where I was in my life.

At night, he got worse. This man got off on making me hot

179

and sweaty. The beads of sweat would drip down my breasts, causing me to remove my clothes at lightning speed. I would get so angry with him because I had spent good money on a blow out, and he would show up and wear me out. Bone straight and laid hair turned into a puffy mini unruly afro. He would have me hot and bothered, waiting to pounce like an animal in heat. What he did to my body tortured me.

Sometimes, I got annoyed and would be cold as ice. I didn't want him here, and I wasn't in the mood to give him the time of day or any loving. He knew exactly what to do to put me on edge and make me cry. He was cruel. I couldn't get wet for him; my girl was bone dry. She wasn't feeling it, and no matter what I did or how hard I tried, she wouldn't cooperate, making sexual matters undesirable.

Foreplay did not work. Normally, breast manipulation gave me pleasure, but he made them sore, and extremely tender which turned me off and killed the mood. It was stressful as fuck. I cannot remember when I last had a good night's sleep. I decided I would definitely need to talk to a professional to help me get rid of this growing problem. Embarrassment and shame made seeking help difficult.

Unfortunately, my mother experienced the same things in her life, and I often went to her for advice. I did not know what to do or how to handle things anymore. My mother gave me expert advice and helped me cope. She became my support system and my rock through these times.

Wondering about the yoyo weight I was experiencing, I asked her if she thought he had anything to do with it. Was I considered fat? Too skinny? I didn't know anymore, and I struggled finding balance.

Unable to focus on any single task, my mind was always scattered and on ten. The trauma that I was dealing with showed up differently each day. Often times, it had me forgetting simple things which dipped my self-esteem lower and lower by the day. *What is wrong with me? Why am I going through this?*

Considering myself a decent person, I felt like I did not deserve this treatment. I felt sick, tired, and frustrated, of the way things was going for me at this time. Life was kicking my ass and he caused all of these feelings. I was doing just fine until he came along.

Reaching out to my mother and confiding in her helped me gain strength. My mother told me that until he left, I should find inner peace and fight my way through this situation. My mother was right; I decided I would ignore him and start living my life with a purpose.

Walking every morning to clear my head and enjoy some me time, I refused to lie in bed depressed. Creating a workout routine forced me to focus on fitness and helped me stay consistent. Fasting on fruits and vegetables two weeks a month would help me keep my weight in check. I doubled down on my water intake, forcing myself to gulp a gallon a day.

Realizing tea kept me calm, I drank a glass daily, and the

warmth ran through my body, giving me a relaxed calm, he could not disturb.

Focused. That's what I was. Living my life with intention.

Braiding my hair in protective styles became my uniform. He could not mess that up. Once it was done, it wasn't going anywhere, and I became less upset when he slid up on me at night, causing me to feel like I worked overtime in a hot factory at the end of the night.

"Hello, my name is Eva."

Deciding to join an online support group, I found comfort in knowing I could talk to other woman experiencing the same things as me without them seeing my face.

Speaking in detail of what I was going through, I poured out my heart to these women, and I never felt judged by them.

"You're not alone, Eva. I have experienced some of the same things as you"

"Girl, I hate to tell you this, but I got it so much worse to the point where I had to seek medical attention."

Listening intently on my newfound community, some of the stories were horrific. I did find comfort in knowing I was not alone.

"How long did you go through this?" I would ask to gauge my situation.

"Ten years," one woman said.

I gasped.

Lord help me, I thought.

After several interactions with the group, the embarrassment and shame slowly left me. I became more open and started asking a lot more questions. Most women gave me great advice and told me ways to cope. A couple of women fortunate to be out of their situations gave me hope.

Gardening became my go to. Placing seeds in the soil and nurturing it until it transformed into something beautiful was so fulfilling for me. Watching food grow from seeds gave my body nourishment that could not be bought.

Cleaning my home became my other saving grace. It was therapeutic and helped me get through tough times. Boiling cinnamon and listening to great music assisted me in making sure my home stayed in order.

Embracing all the tips from my support group really helped me thrive in the situation I was in. I was now living with a purpose. Excited about the next meeting, I decided to turn my camera on.

"Eva!" the ladies yelled.

"You turned your camera on!"

"Yes. I did." Today was the day I would stop hiding, and I refused to keep living a lie. It appeared to everyone that I was alright when I was struggling, going through it, and feeling low. Overcoming so much trauma, I wanted to be transparent, show my face, and live in my truth.

Proud of my new mindset and mental health space, I wanted to show my friends all the peppers, cucumbers, and tomatoes from my garden. Looking better than I had in months, I also wanted to show them that although he was still in and out of my life, I was focused on taking care of myself.

Applauding me and complimenting me during the meeting gave me confidence. I felt strong, and I felt I could handle him head on when he came back around.

Basking in my newfound stability and happiness didn't last long. Out of nowhere, he showed back up, but I didn't let him faze me. I dealt with him as best as I could because I knew he wouldn't be around forever.

At some point, I would be done with my journey through this thing called menopause.

UP THE COAST- IV

I could smell deliciousness from the bed. My beloved was definitely cooking it up for us. As I wrapped myself in her robe and followed my nose out to the dining room, I was not disappointed. Plates of French toast, crispy bacon, and over-easy eggs sat waiting to be devoured. A small bowl with half a grapefruit and glass of cranberry juice sat at each side. She certainly knew how to spoil me.

It was Sunday morning, which always came with its share of frustration at my leaving but also affection as we anticipated my departure until the next weekend. Okoye walked into the dining room with a carafe of juice for refills in her hand.

"Good morning, lover," she said and slid into her chair.

I walked into the room and kissed her on top of her head and smoothed her locs before answering with my own good morning and took my seat. We blessed the food, then started chewing in companionable silence. When I looked up, though, Okoye was staring at me.

"We have to talk."

These words were known to strike fear into relationships, and this one was no different.

"Sure, ok. What's up, boo?"

"I've been doing a lot of reflecting and thinking, and I'm not going to sign the lease renewal."

I looked at her quizzically but didn't stop shoveling food into my mouth. "Why not? I thought this was helping build your credit goals? Do you want somewhere else? I thought you loved this place."

"I do, but what I mean is that I'm not signing another lease with you. I'm moving out and moving on."

I paused with my fork halfway up to my mouth, then put it back down on my plate. I was trying to absorb the information that she was presenting me, but sexy memories of last night, and the two before it, were clouding my understanding. "What do you mean?" I asked her.

"Listen, babe. I know you think I'm a babe in the woods, and I know that I've let you. At some point in my adult life, I've got to accept reality and move forward with my own life. I can't keep putting my life on pause to wait here for you."

"I thought we were happy. My job makes things tough, but it also helps us to be comfortable. Are you breaking up with me because of my job?" My frustration and anger hid the guilt and lies behind them. I was well aware that the job was an enabler to live the lifestyle that I had been maintaining for a little over two years.

"Don't do that. Don't talk to me like I'm stupid. Maybe at first, I allowed myself to be fooled by all the 'social media is too invasive' and 'my schedule' talk, but I've never been dumb. You know that. Do you know how many texts and conversations I've seen and ignored? Do you know how many times you've said Xavier in your sleep? I am well aware that you are still dealing with your baby's father in D.C."

I stared at her, dumbfounded. Why hadn't she said anything? I knew within myself why without even asking. She loved me, and she enjoyed what we were doing.

"Okoye . . ."

"Listen, I love you. I've loved you from the time you stood in my parents living room and promised to take good care of me at University of Miami, even though I didn't even know what it was or what to call it. But I've also got to make a life for myself."

Tears began to fall from my eyes. I had dreaded a conversation like this since the very beginning. I knew I deserved to be berated, raged at, beaten up even. I had been dishonest with her more times than I could count. This calm, decisive talk, though, was far worse. It let me know that nothing would change her mind.

"I'm going to be honest with you. I've been seeing someone for about six months now. He's asked me to move in with him, and I said yes. We're going to get married."

My mouth opened, then closed again without a word. Should I protest? Beg? Argue? What was there even to say? Nothing she said was wrong.

"Listen, Nicolette, I will always love you, but I know you are not mine. I can't keep waiting around to see who you will choose. I had to make a choice for myself. Do you understand?"

I stared at this gorgeous woman before me and suddenly felt more naked in this robe than ever. Remembering her grow from the sweet, shy co-ed who I had met to an accomplished artist, amazing foodie, and self-aware woman, I felt pride mixing in with my heartbreak. I loved Okoye, and love wouldn't allow me to fight for my own interests at her expense.

"Yes, I understand. When will all this take place?"

"I'll be moving throughout the week and expect to turn my keys in by Thursday," she said with finality.

The fact that we usually connected on Thursday nights was not a detail that was lost on me, but I knew not to say anything. So, this was the end. These moments before I got on my plane and headed back to D.C. would be the last moments we had together. I got up from my seat and walked around the table. Without a word, I knelt down on the carpet and placed my head in her lap and cried. She stroked my hair, grabbed my hand, and placed a kiss in my palm.

"Thank you, Nicolette. Thank you for all you have been to me. I will always love you."

"I love you too," I murmured through my sobs, but I knew that it was for the best. Love means that everyone got what they needed. I couldn't believe that she had known all along that Xavier and I were still together, but when I thought back over all the close calls that I thought I had escaped, it was almost insulting to think that she wouldn't.

My flight left just a few hours later, and I left my key on the coffee table, where just a few days ago we were making love and snacking as though these good times would be forever. I tried to pull myself together and regain some resemblance of composure as I headed back to D.C. There was no way I could tell Xavier that my girlfriend had broken up with me—that was definitely not part of our arrangement.

I had already texted ahead to let Xavier know that I would take a car service back to the house because I had some stops to make. Really, I was giving myself a little bit more time for my eyedrops to take the red from my eyes that had cried the entire flight and to wash my face again so that I looked a bit more acceptable.

The house was silent when I walked in, and I thought I had gotten lucky, and he was out or at work. After walking through the foyer and hearing some noise coming from his bedroom, I realized I hadn't gotten that lucky.

"Nicolette, come on in for a sec!" I heard him say. When I walked into the room, he stopped what he was doing and looked at me. I could see four to five suitcases full and zipped all over the room and one bulging on the bed. What the FUCK was going on here?

"Um, Xavier. Are you going somewhere?"

"Yes, Nicolette. I am most decidedly going somewhere." His gaze never left my face.

"Nicolette, I don't know if you remember the fellowship program that I mentioned to you last year. Probably not. It's been super hard to talk to you for at least that long, probably more. But I was accepted and have been working on the program coursework. Now, I am in the clinical phase and going to do my research and action work in Tanzania."

This time, I couldn't hold back the words. "What the FUCK? We're not going all the way to Africa! When did you decide this?"

"You would be right in saying that we are not going to Africa. I have been trying to love you properly for more years than I can count. You never let me in; you never wanted to have anything beyond the parenting and physical for us. That's not what I want anymore, Nicolette. I want someone to enjoy being with me and appreciate all of me. I finally had to come to terms with the fact that we would never have that and I don't want to force it if that's not what you want."

My mouth stood open but wordless for the second time that day. Were these two talking to each other? This was unbelievable.

Since I didn't say anything, he continued. "You know that you are welcome to stay here as long as you like. I would never put the mother of my son out on the street, but I need you to know that I plan on making this an extended trip, and I don't know when or if I will be back. Zay is going to join me over his summer vacation, and then he will head back to start as a Bison in September." I wanted to be incredulous that my own son hadn't mentioned his plans to me, but then I remembered that I had been rather self-absorbed for the past few months at least juggling my lovers.

I was rooted in this spot, unable to move, simply trying to absorb what he was saying. Unexpectedly, I rushed to his arms and wrapped mine around him in a hug.

"It's ok. It's ok. I know you'll be fine. You're a trooper," he murmured into my hair as he returned my embrace. He kissed the top of my head, then held me out at arm's length. Looking into his eyes this time, I could tell that this was the end.

The next day, I watched him roll his suitcases out the door with the help of the driver and looked at his mostly empty room. It reflected what I felt: empty inside. The two lovers, who I had spent so much of my time and focus on were so swiftly and decisively removed from my life. I felt like I should have been broken, but instead, I just felt tired.

No work today. I was going to spend this day in healing. My thoughts had been swirling around all that I had experienced. Xavier was right. I was a trooper; I was going to be alright. I had been using Xavier and Okoye as security blankets in different ways for far too long. It was time for me to step up and be the woman who I needed to be. It was time for me to give myself a chance at life and love without all the barriers I had put in place.

The silence in the big house was deafening. I picked up the phone and dialed one of my favorite sources of strength and understanding.

"Hey, auntie! I think I'm gonna come and visit with you for a few days. Is that ok?"

ABOUT THE AUTHORS

Delia Rouse grew up in Brooklyn, New York. Growing up she was fascinated with people watching and day dreaming which led to an early exposure of reading and creating stories. Delia has an English Communications degree from North Carolina Central University and resides in Raleigh, North Carolina with her husband and 2 daughters.

ABOUT THE AUTHORS

Nicole Newman has been a collector of words since listening to stories on her parents' laps. She finally has worked to take ownership of their arrangement as an authentic author. This is her 3rd collaborative writing project. Nicole is a career educator from South Bend, Indiana living in Dallas, TX with her husband of 22 years and their four children.

Contact Delia Nicole:

Delia Nicole

@Delianicolebook

delianicolebooks

delianicolebooks@gmail.com

Like, Follow, and Share to get the latest news, release info, and content from authors Delia Nicole!

Made in the USA
Coppell, TX
28 August 2021